"I've applied for a special license. We'll get married here in forty-eight hours."

Polly toppled back onto the sofa again, a look of complete astonishment fixed to her startled face. "Say that again—"

"You have made it clear that you will not accept any other options," Raul drawled flatly.

"But I never expected...I mean, f-for goodness' sake, Raul," Polly stammered in severe shock. "We can't just—"

"Can't we? Are you about to change your mind? Are you now prepared to consider allowing me to take my child back home with me?"

Dear Reader,

What I enjoy most about writing is the creation of entirely different heroines. THE HUSBAND HUNTERS is about three women who find love where they least expect it. Maxie cannot imagine any man appreciating her for herself, rather than for her looks. Darcy has been badly hurt and has given up on the male sex. Polly falls in love and is betrayed. To match these ladies, we have Angelos, who fondly imagines that Maxie will be his the instant he asks, Luca, who seeks revenge by ensuring that Darcy marries no one but him, and Raul, who finds out the hard way that Polly, the idealistic mother of his child, can be surprisingly unforgiving....

Yours sincerely,

*Lynne Graham*

# LYNNE GRAHAM

## Contract Baby

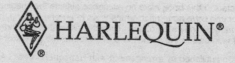

TORONTO • NEW YORK • LONDON
AMSTERDAM • PARIS • SYDNEY • HAMBURG
STOCKHOLM • ATHENS • TOKYO • MILAN • MADRID
PRAGUE • WARSAW • BUDAPEST • AUCKLAND

ISBN 0-373-12013-3

CONTRACT BABY

First North American Publication 1999.

Copyright © 1998 by Lynne Graham.

All rights reserved. Except for use in any review, the reproduction or
utilization of this work in whole or in part in any form by any electronic,
mechanical or other means, now known or hereafter invented, including
xerography, photocopying and recording, or in any information storage
or retrieval system, is forbidden without the written permission of the
publisher, Harlequin Enterprises Limited, 225 Duncan Mill Road,
Don Mills, Ontario, Canada M3B 3K9.

All characters in this book have no existence outside the imagination of
the author and have no relation whatsoever to anyone bearing the same
name or names. They are not even distantly inspired by any individual
known or unknown to the author, and all incidents are pure invention.

This edition published by arrangement with Harlequin Books S.A.

® and TM are trademarks of the publisher. Trademarks indicated with
® are registered in the United States Patent and Trademark Office, the
Canadian Trade Marks Office and in other countries.

Printed in U.S.A.

# CHAPTER ONE

FROM the slim document case clasped in one strong brown hand, Raul Zaforteza withdrew a large glossy photograph. 'This is Polly Johnson. In six weeks' time she will give birth to my child. I *must* find her before then.'

Somehow primed to expect a gorgeous blonde with a supermodel face and figure, Digby was disconcerted to find himself looking at a small, slim girl with a mane of hair the colour of mahogany, soulful blue eyes and an incredibly sweet smile. She looked so outrageously young and wholesome he just could not imagine her in the role of surrogate mother.

As a lawyer with a highly respected London firm, Digby Carson had dealt with some very difficult cases. But a surrogacy arrangement gone wrong? The surrogate mother on the run and probably determined to keep the baby? He surveyed his most wealthy and influential client with a sinking heart.

Raul Zaforteza's fabled fortune was founded on gold and diamond mines. He was a brilliant business tycoon, a legendary polo player and, according to the gossip columns, a notorious womaniser. He was already prowling like a black panther ready to spring. Six feet two inches tall, with the sleek, supple build of a born athlete and the volatile temperament of his colourful heritage, he was an intimidating sight, even to a man who had known him from childhood.

'Digby...I understood that my lawyer in New York had already briefed you on this situation,' Raul drawled with barely concealed impatience.

'He said the matter was far too confidential to discuss on the phone. And I hadn't the slightest suspicion that you were planning to become a father through surrogacy,' the older man admitted. 'Why on earth did you embark on such a risky venture?'

'*Por Dios*...you watched me grow up! How can you ask me that?' Raul countered.

Digby looked uncomfortable. As a former employee of Raul's late father, he was well aware that Raul had had a pretty ghastly childhood. He might be rich beyond avarice, but he had not been anything like as lucky in the parent lottery.

His bronzed features taut, Raul expelled his breath in a slow hiss. 'I decided a long time ago that I would never marry. I wouldn't give any woman that amount of power over me *or*, even more crucially, over any child we might have!' Fierce conviction roughened his rich, accented drawl. 'But I've always been very fond of children—'

'Yes...' An unspoken *but* hovered in the tense silence.

'Many marriages end in divorce, and usually the wife gets to keep the children,' Raul reminded the lawyer with biting cynicism. 'Surrogacy impressed me as the most practical way in which to father a child outside marriage. This wasn't an impulsive decision, Digby. When I decided to go ahead, I went to a lot of trouble to ensure that I would choose a suitable mother for my child.'

'Suitable?' Digby was keen to hear what Raul, with his famed love of fast, glitzy society blondes, had considered 'suitable' in the maternal stakes.

'When my New York legal team advertised for a surrogate mother, they received a flood of applications. I employed a doctor and a psychologist to put a shortlist of the more promising candidates through a battery of tests, but the responsibility for the final choice was naturally mine.'

The older man frowned down at the photograph of Polly Johnson. 'What age is she?'

'Twenty-one.'

Digby's frown remained. 'She was the *only* suitable candidate?'

Raul tautened. 'The psychologist did have some reservations but I decided to overlook them.'

Digby looked shaken.

'Everything that the psychologist saw in Polly I *wanted* in the mother of my child,' Raul stressed without a shade of regret. 'It was a gut feeling and I acted on it. Yes, she was young and idealistic, but she had the right moral values. She wasn't motivated by greed but by a desperate need to try and finance surgery which she hoped might extend her mother's life.'

'I wonder how that desperation affected her ability to make a rational decision about what she was getting involved in,' Digby remarked.

'Wondering is a pointless exercise now that she is pregnant with my child,' Raul countered very drily. 'But I *will* find her soon. Her background was exhaustively investigated. I now know that, just two months ago, she was at her godmother's home in Surrey. I don't yet know where she went from there. But before I do find her I need to know what my rights are in this country.'

Digby was in no hurry to break bad news before he had all the facts. British law frowned on surrogacy. If the mother wanted to keep the baby instead of handing it over, no contract was likely to persuade a British judge that taking that child from its mother was in the child's best interests.

'Tell me the rest of the story,' he advised.

While running through the bare facts for the older man's benefit, Raul stared unseeingly out of the window, grimly recalling his first sight of Polly Johnson through a two-way mirror in the New York legal office. She had reminded him of a tiny porcelain doll. Fragile, unusual and astonishingly pretty.

She had been brave and honest. And so impressively *nice*—not something Raul had ever sought in a woman before, but a trait he had found very appealing when he had considered all the positive qualities a mother might hand down to her child. Certainly Polly had been younger and less worldly wise than was desirable, but he had recognised her quiet inner strength as well as her essentially tranquil nature.

And the more Raul had watched Polly, the more he had learnt about Polly, the more he had wanted to *meet* Polly face to face, in the flesh, so that some day in the future he could comfortably answer his child's curious questions about her. But his New York lawyer had said absolutely not. Strict anonymity would be his only defence against any form of harassment in later years. But Raul had always been a ruthless rule-breaker, with immense faith in his own natural instincts, nor had he ever hesitated to satisfy his own wishes...

And acting on that essential arrogance, he conceded grudgingly now, was how everything had begun to fall apart. Worst of all, he who prided himself on his intelligence and his shrewd perceptive powers had somehow failed to notice the warning signs of trouble on the horizon.

'So once you knew that the girl had successfully conceived, you installed her in a house in Vermont with a trusted family servant to look after her,' Digby recapped, because Raul had fallen silent again. 'Where was her mother while all this was going on?'

'As soon as Polly signed the contract her mother went into a convalescent home to build up her strength for surgery. She was very ill. The woman knew nothing about the surrogacy agreement. When Polly was only a couple of weeks pregnant, her mother had the operation. Polly had been warned that her mother's chances of survival were at best only even. She died two days after surgery,' Raul revealed heavily.

'Unfortunate.'

Raul slung him a fulminating glance of scorn. *Unfortunate?* Polly had been devastated. And Raul had been uneasily conscious that her sole reason for becoming a surrogate had died that same day. Aware from the frustratingly brief reports made by the maid, Soledad, that Polly was deeply depressed, Raul had reached the point where he could no longer bear to stay at a supposedly sensible distance from the woman carrying his baby.

Understandably he had been concerned that she might miscarry. He had sincerely believed that it was his responsibility to offer her support. Isolated in a country that wasn't her own, only twenty-one-years old, pregnant with a stranger's baby and plunged deep into a grieving process that her optimistic outlook had not prepared her to face, the mother of his child had really *needed* a sympathetic shoulder.

'So I finally made contact with her,' Raul admitted tautly. 'Since I could hardly admit that I was the father of her baby, I had to employ a certain amount of deception to make that contact.'

Unseen, Digby winced. Raul should have avoided any form of personal involvement. But then Raul Zaforteza was a disturbingly complex man. He was a merciless business opponent and a very dangerous enemy. More than one woman had come to grief on the rocks of his innate emotional detachment. But Raul was also a renowned philanthropist, the most genuine of friends to a chosen few and a male still capable of powerful emotional responses.

Raul compressed his firm lips. 'I took a weekend place near where she was staying and ensured that our paths crossed. I didn't conceal my identity; I didn't need to...the Zaforteza name meant nothing to her. Over the following months, I flew up there regularly and called on her. I never stayed long...she just needed someone to talk to.' Radiating tension now, in spite of that studiously nonchalant explanation, Raul shrugged, his accented drawl petering out into another brooding silence.

'*And?*'

'And nothing!' As he swung round from the window, Raul's hard, dark eyes were sardonic in their comprehension. 'I treated her like a little sister. I was a casual visitor, nothing more.'

Digby restrained himself from pointing out that since Raul was an only child he could only have the vaguest notion of how one treated a little sister. And Digby had three daughters, every one of whom swooned at the mere mention of Raul's name. Indeed, the last time he had taken Raul home for dinner it had been a downright embarrassing experience, with all three daughters dressed to kill and competing for Raul's attention. Even his wife said that Raul Zaforteza might well have been packaged by the devil specifically to tempt the female sex.

He pictured a lonely young woman who might only have faced up to what surrogacy really *meant* in the aftermath of her mother's death. When that nice, naive young woman had suddenly found herself entertaining a member of the international jet set as self-assured, sophisticated and charismatic as Raul, what effect had it had on her?

'When did she go missing?' Digby prompted.

'Three months ago. She disappeared one day... Soledad went out shopping and left her alone,' Raul confided grimly. 'Do you realize that in three months I have hardly slept a night through? Day *and* night I have been worried sick—'

'I suppose there *is* a strong possibility that she may have gone for a termination—'

'*Por Dios...*' Raul dealt the older man a smouldering look of reproof. 'Polly wouldn't abort my child!'

Content to have issued that warning, Digby didn't argue.

'Polly's very soft, very feminine, very caring...she would *never* choose that option!' Raul continued to argue fiercely.

'You asked about your rights.' Digby breathed in deep, straightening his shoulders to brace himself for the blow he was about to deliver. 'I'm afraid unmarried fathers don't have any under British law.'

Raul stared back at him with rampant incredulity. 'That isn't possible.'

'You couldn't argue that the girl would make a bad mother either. After all, you *chose* her,' the older man pointed out ruefully. 'You described a respectable girl, drawn into a surrogacy agreement only because she was trying to help her mother. As the rich foreigner who used his wealth to tempt her into making a decision which she later regretted, you wouldn't look good in court—'

'But she has reneged on a legal contract,' Raul spelt out harshly. '*Dios mio!* All I want is the right to take my own child back to Venezuela. I haven't the slightest desire to take this into a courtroom! There has to be some other way in which I can get custody.'

Digby grimaced. 'You *could* marry her…'

Raul gave him a forbidding look. 'If that was a joke, Digby…it was in the worst possible taste.'

Henry pulled out a chair for Polly to sit down to her evening meal. His mother, Janice Grey, frowned at the young woman's shadowed blue eyes and too prominent cheekbones. At eight months pregnant, Polly looked drawn and ill.

'You should be resting at this stage of your pregnancy,' Janice reproved. 'If you married Henry now, you could give up work. You could take things easy while he helped you get your godmother's will sorted out.'

'It would be the best move you could make.' Solid and bespectacled, with thinning fair hair, Henry nodded in pompous agreement. 'You'll have to be careful that the Inland Revenue doesn't take too large a slice of your inheritance.'

'I really don't want to marry anybody.' Beneath her wealth of rich, reddish brown hair, Polly's delicate features were becoming stiff and her smile strained.

An awkward silence fell while mother and son exchanged meaningful glances.

Polly focused on her nicely cooked meal with a guilty

lack of appetite. It had been a mistake to take a room in Janice's comfortable terraced home. But how could she ever have guessed that her late godmother's trusted house-keeper had had an ulterior motive for offering her somewhere to stay?

Janice and her son *knew* the strange terms of Nancy Leeward's will. They *knew* that Polly would inherit a million pounds if she found a husband within the year and stayed married for at least six months. Janice was determined to persuade Polly that marrying her son would magically solve her every problem.

And, to be fair to Janice, calculating she might be, but she saw such a marriage as a fair exchange. After all, Polly was an unmarried mum-to-be and couldn't claim her godmother's money without a husband. Henry was single, and in a job he loathed. Even a small share of a million pounds would enable Henry to set up as a tax consultant in a smart office of his own. Janice would do just about anything to further Henry's prospects, and Henry wasn't just attached to his widowed mother's apron strings, he was welded to them.

'Babies can be very demanding,' Janice pointed out when her son had left the room. 'And, talking as someone who has done it, raising a child alone isn't easy.'

'I know.' But at the mere mention of the word 'baby' a vague and dreamy smile had formed on Polly's face. There was nothing practical or sensible about the warm feeling of anticipation which welled up inside her.

Janice sighed. 'I'm only trying to advise you, Polly. You're not in love with Henry, but where did falling in love get you?'

Polly's blissful abstraction was cruelly punctured by that reminder. 'Nowhere,' she conceded tightly.

'I've never liked to pry, but it's obvious that the father of your child took off the minute you got pregnant. Unreliable and irresponsible,' the older woman opined thinly. 'You certainly couldn't call my Henry either of those things.'

Polly considered Henry's joyless and stolid outlook on life and suppressed a sigh.

'People don't always marry for love. People get married for all sorts of other reasons,' Janice persisted. 'Security, companionship, a nice home.'

'I'm afraid I would need more.' Polly got up slowly and heavily. 'I think I'll lie down for a while before I go to work.'

Breathless from climbing the stairs, Polly lay down on her bed in the prettily furnished spare room. She grimaced. Never in a million years would she marry Henry just to satisfy the terms of Nancy Leeward's will and inherit that money.

She was too shamefully conscious that a craving for money had reduced her to her present predicament. Her late father, a strongly religious man, had been fond of saying that money was the root of all evil. And, looking back to the twisted, reckless decision she had made months earlier, Polly knew that in her case that pronouncement had proved all too true.

Her mother had been dying. But Polly had refused to accept the reality that the mother she had grown up without and had barely had time to get to know again *could* be dying: she hadn't believed the hand of fate could be that cruel. Armed by that stubborn belief, Polly had gone that extra mile that people talked about, but she had gone that extra mile in entirely the wrong direction, she acknowledged wretchedly.

How could she *ever* have believed that she would find it possible to give her baby up to strangers? How could she *ever* have imagined that she could surrender all rights, hand over her own flesh and blood and agree never, ever to try and see her own child again? She had been incredibly stupid and immature. So she had run away from a situation which had become untenable, knowing even then that she would be followed and eventually *traced*...

As the ever-present threat of being found and called to account for her behaviour assailed Polly, her skin turned clammy with fear. In her own mind she was no better than a criminal. She had signed a contract in which she had promised to give up her baby. She had sat back while an unbelievably huge amount of money was expended on her mother's medical care and then she had fled. She had broken the law, yet she had been wickedly and savagely deceived into signing that contract...but what proof did she have of that fact?

Sometimes she woke from nightmares about being extradited to the USA and put on trial, her baby taken from her and parcelled off to a life of luxury with his immoral and utterly unscrupulous father in Venezuela. Even when she didn't have bad dreams, it was becoming increasingly hard to sleep. She was at that point in pregnancy when she couldn't get comfortable even in bed, and she was often wakened by the strong, energetic movements of her baby.

And in her mind's eye then, when she was at her weakest, she would see Raul. Raul Zaforteza, dark, devastating and dangerous. What a trusting and pathetic victim she had been! For she had fallen in love with him, hopelessly, helplessly, blindly in love for the first time in her life. She had lived only from one meeting to the next, frantically counting the days in between, agonised if he didn't turn up and always tormented by the secret she had believed she was still contriving to keep from him. A jagged laugh was torn from her lips now. And all the time Raul had known she was pregnant. After all, he was the father of her baby...

An hour later, Polly headed to work. It was a cool, wet summer evening. She walked past the bus stop. She was presently struggling to save every penny she could. Soon she wouldn't be able to work any more, and once she had the baby she would need her savings for all sorts of things.

The supermarket where she worked shifts was a bright beacon of light and activity in the city street. As Polly disposed of her coat and her bag in the rest room, the manageress popped her head round the door and frowned. 'You look very tired, Polly. I hope that doctor of yours knows what he's doing when he tells you that it's all right for you to be still working.'

Polly flushed as the older woman withdrew again. She hadn't actually seen a doctor in two months, but at her last visit she had been advised to rest. How could she rest when she had to keep herself? And if she approached the social services for assistance they would ask too many awkward questions. So she lived in a state of permanent exhaustion, back aching, ankles swollen, and if she pushed herself too hard she got blinding headaches and dizzy spells.

By the end of her shift on one of the checkouts Polly was very tired, and really grateful that she was off the next day. Tomorrow, she decided, she would pamper herself. Shouldering her bag, she left the shop. The rain had stopped. The street lights gleamed off the wet pavements and cars swished by splashing the kerbs.

Polly didn't even try to close her coat. Only a tent would have closed round her swollen stomach, and the weight of her own body contributed to her fatigue. Not long now, she consoled herself. She felt as if she had been pregnant for ever, but soon she would be getting to know her baby as a separate little person.

Engaged in her thoughts of the near future, head downbent, Polly didn't register the existence of a large obstacle in her path. Only at the last possible moment, when she almost cannoned into the impossibly tall and solidly built male blocking her passage, did she notice the presence of another human being and seek to sidestep him.

As she teetered dangerously off balance, a cry of dismay escaping her, a pair of strong hands shot out to catch her by the shoulders and steady her. Heart pounding with fright, she reeled as he held her there, her head tipping back from a view of her rescuer's silver-grey silk tie to look up.

Raul Zaforteza gazed down at her from his great height, his facial muscles locking his staggeringly handsome features into a bronze mask of impassivity that was uniquely chilling.

In severe shock, Polly trembled, soft mouth opening and closing again without sound, a look of pure panic in her gaze as she collided with eyes that had the topaz golden brilliance of a tiger ready to claw the unwary to the bone.

'There is no place in this whole wide world where you could hope to stay hidden from me,' Raul spelt out in a controlled tone of immense finality, his rich, accented vowel sounds tingling in her sensitive ears, throwing up a myriad of despoilt memories that could only torment her. 'The chase is over.'

# CHAPTER TWO

'LET me go, Raul!' Polly gasped convulsively, her heart thudding like a trapped animal's behind her breastbone, nervous perspiration beading her short upper lip.

'How can I do that?' Raul countered with level emphasis. 'You're expecting my baby. What sort of a man *could* walk away?'

Without warning, pain flashed in a scorching burst across Polly's temples, provoking a startled moan from her parted lips. Her hand flew up to press against her throbbing brow. Nausea stirred nastily in her stomach as the overpowering dizziness washed over her.

'*Por Dios*...what is the matter with you?' Raul tightened his hold on her as she swayed like a drunk, straining with every sinew to stay upright and in control.

In another moment he bent and swept her up into his arms, cradling her easily into the strength and heat of his big, powerful frame. As the street light shone on the greyish pallor of her upturned face, Raul emitted a groan and said something hoarse in Spanish.

'Put me down...' Polly was not too ill to appreciate the cruel irony of Raul getting that physically close to her for the very first time.

Ignoring her, chiselled profile aggressively clenched, Raul jerked his imperious dark head and the limousine parked across the street filtered over to the kerb. The chauffeur jumped out and hurried to open the passenger door. Raul settled her down on the squashy leather back seat, but before he could climb in beside her Polly took him by surprise and lurched half out again, to be violently sick in the

17

gutter. Then she sagged back on the seat, pressing a tissue
to her tremulous lips and utterly drained.

As she lay slumped on her side, a stunned silence greeted
her. Momentarily, a dull gleam of amusement touched her.
Raul Zaforteza had probably got to the age of thirty-one
without ever having witnessed such a distasteful event. And
she hated him for being there to witness her inability to
control her own body. Although she was the kind of person
who automatically said sorry when other people bumped
into *her*, a polite apology would have choked her.

'Do you feel strong enough to sit up?'

As she braced a slender hand on the seat beneath her,
Raul took over, raising her and propping her up like a rag
doll. Involuntarily she breathed in the elusive scent of him.
Clean, warm male overlaid with a hint of something more
exotic.

'So you finally ran me to earth,' Polly acknowledged
curtly, refusing to look at him, staring into space with almost blank blue eyes.

'It was only a matter of time. I went first to the house
where you're staying. Janice Grey wasn't helpful.
Fortunately I was already aware of where you worked,'
Raul imparted flatly.

She could feel the barrier between them, high and impenetrable as toughened frosted glass, the highwire tension
splintering through the atmosphere, the restive, brooding
edge of powerful energy that Raul always emanated. But
*she* felt numb, like an accident victim. He had found her.
She had made every possible effort to remain undetected—
moved to London, even lied to friends so that nobody had
a contact address or phone number for her. And all those
endeavours had been in vain.

As a spasm of pain afflicted her, she squeezed her eyes
tight shut.

'What *is* it?' Raul demanded fiercely.

'Feel like my head's splitting open,' she mumbled sickly,
forcing her eyes open again.

Raul was now studying the pronounced swell of her stomach with a shaken fascination that felt deeply, offensively intrusive.

In turn, Polly now studied him, pain like a poisonous dart piercing her bruised heart. His hair—black as midnight now, but blue-black in sunlight—the strong, flaring ebony brows, the lean, arrogant nose, the magnificent high cheekbones and hollows, the wide, perfectly modelled mouth so eloquent of the raw sensuality that laced his every movement. A devastatingly attractive male, so staggeringly good-looking he had to turn heads wherever he went, and yet only the most audacious woman would risk cornering him. There was reinforced steel in those hard bones, inflexible control in that strong jawline.

The baby kicked, blanking out her mind, making her wince.

His incongruously long and lush black lashes swept up, and she was pinned to the spot by glinting gold eyes full of enquiry.

'May I?' he murmured almost roughly.

And then she saw his half-extended hand, those lean brown fingers full of such tensile strength, and only after a split second did she register in shock the source of his interest. His entire attention was on the giant mound of her stomach, a strangely softened expression driving the tension from his firm lips.

'May I feel my child move?' he clarified boldly.

Polly gave him a stricken look of condemnation, and with shaking, frantic hands tried somewhat pointlessly to try and yank her coat over herself. 'Don't you *dare* try to touch me!'

'Perhaps you are wise. Perhaps touching is not a good idea.' Nostrils flaring, Raul flung himself back in the corner of the seat, hooded eyes betraying only a chilling glint of intent gold, his bronzed face cold as a guillotine, impassive now in icy self-restraint.

And yet Polly was reminded of nothing so much as a

wild animal driven into ferocious retreat. He had never looked at her like that in Vermont, but she had always sensed the primal passion of the temperament he restrained. Then, as now, it had exercised the most terrifying fascination for her—a male her complete opposite in nature, an outwardly civilised sophisticate in mannerism, speech and behaviour, but at heart never, ever cool, predictable or tranquil.

'Take me home,' she muttered tightly. 'I'll meet you tomorrow to talk.'

He lifted the phone and spoke in fluid Spanish to his driver. Polly turned away.

She remembered him in Vermont, addressing Soledad in Spanish. She remembered the maid's nervous unease, her undeniable servility. When Raul had been around, Soledad had tried to melt into the woodwork, too unsophisticated a woman to handle the cruel complexity of the situation he had unthinkingly put her in. In his eyes she had only been a servant after all. Raul Zaforteza was not a male accustomed to taking account of the needs or the feelings of lesser beings...and in Soledad's case he had paid a higher price than he would ever know for that arrogance.

The powerful car drew away from the kerb and shot Polly's flailing and confused thoughts back to the present. While Raul employed the car phone to make a lengthy call in Spanish, she watched him helplessly from below her lashes. She scanned the width of his shoulders under the superb fit of his charcoal-grey suit, the powerful chest, lean hips and long muscular thighs that not the most exquisite tailoring in the world could conceal.

'*I* can't touch *you* but every look you give me is a visual assault,' Raul derided in a whiplash aside as he replaced the phone. 'I'd eat you for breakfast, little girl!'

Her temples throbbed and she closed her eyes, shaken that he could speak to her like that. So many memories washed over her that she was cast into turmoil. Raul, tender, laughing, amber eyes warm as the kiss of sunlight, without a shade of coldness. And every bit of that caring concern aimed at the ultimate well-being of the baby in her womb, at the physical body cocooning his child *not* at Polly personally. She had never existed for him on any level except as a human incubator to be kept calm, content and healthy. But how could she ever have guessed that shattering truth?

'You look terrible,' Raul informed her tautly. 'You've lost a lot of weight and you were very slim to begin with—'

'Nobody could ever accuse me of that now.'

'Your ankles are swollen.'

Polly rested her pounding head back wearily, beyond caring about what she must look like to him now. It scarcely mattered. She had been ten times more presentable in Vermont and he had not been remotely attracted to her, although she had only recognised that humiliating reality in retrospect. 'You're not getting my baby,' she warned him doggedly. 'Not under any circumstances.'

'Calm yourself,' Raul commanded deflatingly. 'Anxiety won't improve your health.'

'*It* always comes first, right?' Polly could not resist sniping.

'*Desde luego*...of course,' Raul confirmed without hesitation.

She winced as another dull flash of pain made her very brain ache. She heard him open a compartment, the hiss of a bottle cap released, liquid tinkling into a glass, and finally another unrecognisable sound. And then she jerked in astonishment when an ice-cold cloth was pressed against her pulsing brow.

'I will take care of you now. Did I not do so before? And look at you now, like a living corpse...' Raul condemned, his dark drawl alive with fierce undertones as he bent over her. 'I wanted to shout at you. I wanted to make you tremble. But how can I do *that* when you are like this?'

Her curling lashes lifted. Defenceless in pain, she stared up into frustrated and furious golden eyes so nakedly at

variance with the compassionate gesture of that cool, soothing cloth he had drenched for her benefit. Being kind to
her was killing him. She understood that. Suffering that
grudging kindness was killing *her*.

'You taught me to *hate*,' she whispered, with a sudden
ferocity alien to her gentle nature until that moment.

The stunning eyes veiled to a slumberous gleam. 'There
is nothing between us but my baby. *No* other connection,
*nada más*...nothing more,' he stressed with gritty exacti-
tude. 'Only when you can detach yourself from your emotional mindset and recall that contract will we talk.'

Hatred flamed like a shooting star through Polly. She
needed it. She needed hatred to race like adrenalin through
her veins. Only hatred could swallow up and ease the ago-
nizing pain Raul could inflict.

'You bastard,' Polly muttered shakily. 'You lying, cheating, devious bastard...'

At that precise moment the limo came to a smooth halt.
As the chauffeur climbed out, Polly gaped at the well-lit
modern building with its beautifully landscaped frontage
outside which the car had drawn up. 'Where are we?' she
demanded apprehensively.

A uniformed nurse emerged from the entrance with a
wheelchair.

In silence Raul swung out of the limo and strode round
the bonnet to wave away the hovering chauffeur. He
opened the door beside her himself.

'You need medical attention,' he delivered.

Her shaken eyes widened, filling with instantaneous fear.
Not for nothing had she visited the library to learn all she
could from newspapers about Raul Zaforteza's ruthless
reputation. 'You're not banging me up in some lunatic asy-
lum!' she flung in complete panic.

'Curb your wild imagination, *chica*. I would do nothing
to harm the mother of my child. And don't you *dare* try to
cause a scene when my only concern is for your well-
being!' Raul warned with ferocious bite as he leant in and

scooped her still resisting body out of the luxurious car as
if she weighed no more than a feather.

'The wheelchair, sir,' the nurse proffered.

'She weighs nothing. I'll carry her.' Raul strode through
the automatic doors, clutching her with the tense concern
of someone handling a particular fragile parcel. *The mother
of his child.* Cue for reverent restraint, she reflected bitterly.
Restraint and concern that the human incubator should be
proving less than efficient. But, weak and sick from pain,
even her vision blurring, she rested her head down against
a broad shoulder.

'Hate you,' she muttered nonetheless, and would have
told him that with her last dying breath because it was her
only defence.

'You're not tough enough to hate,' Raul dismissed as a
grey-haired older man in a white coat moved towards them.

Raul addressed him in a flood of Spanish. Scanning her
with frowning eyes, the doctor led the way into a plush
consulting room on the ground floor.

'Why does nobody speak English? We're in London,'
Polly moaned.

'I'm sorry. Rodney Bevan is a consultant who worked
for many years in a clinic of mine in Venezuela. I can talk
faster in my own language.' Raul laid her down carefully
on a comfortable treatment couch.

'Go away now,' Polly urged him feverishly.

Raul stayed put. The consultant said something quiet in
Spanish. Raul's blunt cheekbones were accentuated by a
faint line of dark colour. He swung on his heel and strode
out to the waiting area, closing the door behind him.

'What did you say?' Polly was impressed to death.

As the waiting nurse moved forward to help Polly out
of her coat, the older man smiled. 'You're the star here,
not him.'

The nurse took her blood pressure. Why were their faces
so solemn? Was there something wrong with her blood

pressure? Her body felt like a great weight pulling her down.

'You need to relax and keep calm, Polly,' the doctor murmured. 'I want to give you a mild sedative and then I would like to scan you. Is that all right with you?'

'No, I want to go home,' she mumbled fearfully, knowing she sounded like a child and not caring, because she didn't feel she could trust anybody so friendly with Raul.

The voices went away. Raul's rich, dark drawl broke into her frantic barely half-formed thoughts. 'Polly... *please* let the medics do what they need to do,' he urged.

She forced her eyes open, focusing on him with difficulty, seeing those lean bronzed features through a blur. 'I can't trust you... or them... you *know* him!'

And even in the state she was in she saw him react in shock to that frightened accusation. Raul turned pale, the fabulous bone structure clenching hard. He gripped her hand, brilliant eyes shimmering. 'You *must* trust him. He's a very fine obstetrician—'

'He's a friend of yours.'

'*Sí, pero*... yes, but he is also a *doctor*,' Raul stressed with highly emotive urgency.

'I don't want to go to sleep and wake up in Venezuela... Do you think I don't know what you're capable of when you're crossed?' Polly managed to frame with the last of her energy.

'I've never broken the law!'

'You *would* to get this baby,' Polly told him.

The silence smouldered, fireworks blazing under the surface.

Raul stared down at her, expressive eyes veiled, but she knew she had drawn blood.

'You're not well, Polly. If you will not believe my assurances that you can trust the staff here, then at least think of the baby's needs and put those needs first,' he breathed, not quite levelly.

A pained look of withdrawal crossed her exhausted face.

She gave a jerky nod of assent, but turned her head to the wall. A minute later she felt a slight prick in her arm and she let herself float, and would have done anything to escape that relentless pounding inside her skull and forget that unjust look of cruel reproach she had seen in Raul's gaze.

As she drifted like a drowning swimmer, all the worst moments of her life seemed to flash up before her.

Her earliest memory was of her father shouting at her mother and her mother crying. She had got up one morning at the age of seven to find her mother gone. Her father had flown into a rage when she'd innocently tried to question him. Soon after that she had been sent to stay with her godmother. Nancy Leeward had carefully explained. Her mother, Leah, had done a very silly thing: she had gone away with another man. Her parents were getting a divorce, but some time, hopefully soon, when her father gave permission, her mother might come to visit her.

Only Leah never had. Polly had got her mothering from her godmother. And she had had to wait until she was twenty years old and clearing out her father's desk, days after his funeral, to discover the pitiful wad of pleading letters written by the distraught mother who had to all intents and purposes abandoned her.

Leah had gone to New York and eventually married her lover. She had flown over to England half a dozen times, at an expense she could ill afford, in repeated attempts to see her daughter, but her embittered ex-husband had blocked her every time—not least by putting Polly into boarding school and refusing to say where she was. Polly had been shattered by what she'd uncovered, but also overjoyed to realise that her mother had really loved her, in spite of all her father's assertions to the contrary.

In New York, she had had a tearful, wonderful reunion with Leah, whose second husband had died the previous year. Her mother had been weak, breathless, and aged far beyond her years. The gravity of her heart condition had been painfully obvious. She had been living on welfare, what health insurance she had had exhausted. The harassed doctor at the local clinic had reluctantly told Polly under pressure that there *was* an operation performed by a world-famous surgeon which might give her mother some hope, but that it would take a lottery win to privately finance such major surgery.

Up, down—too much down in her life recently, and not enough up, she thought painfully as she wandered through her own memories.

And then she saw Raul, strolling through the glorious Vermont woods where she had walked every day, escaping from Soledad's kind but fussing attentions to cry in peace for the mother she had lost. Raul, garbed in faultlessly cut casual clothes, smart enough to take Rodeo Drive by storm and so smooth, so impressively natural in his surprise at stumbling on her that it was a wonder he hadn't cut himself with his own clever tongue.

And she had met those extraordinary eyes of amber and bang...crash...*pow*. She had been heading for a down that would take her all the way to hell, even though she had naively felt she was on an up the instant he angled that first smouldering smile at her.

Polly woke up the following morning wearing a hideous billowing hospital gown. She had a room to herself with a private bathroom. Her head no longer hurt, but tiredness still filled her with lethargy.

The nurse who came in response to the bell cheerfully ran through routine checks, efficiently helped her to freshen up and neatly side-stepped most of her anxious questions. She consulted her chart and informed Polly that she was to have complete bedrest. Mr. Bevan would be in around lunchtime, she confided, just as breakfast was delivered.

A couple of hours later Raul's chauffeur arrived, like an advance party before him. He settled down a suitcase that Polly recognised because it was her own. The case bulged

with what struck her as very probably every possession she
had last seen in her room at the Greys'. A maid in an
overall came in and helped her change into one of her own
nighties. Polly then retrieved a creased brown envelope
from the jumble of items in the foot of her case. It was
time to confront Raul with the worst of the deceptions prac-
tised on her.

By the time mid-morning arrived, Polly was sitting bolt
upright with wide, angrily impatient eyes and, had she but
known it, the first healthy colour in her cheeks for weeks.
She raked restive fingers through the silky mahogany hair
tumbling round her shoulders and focused on the door expectantly, like someone not only preparing to face
Armageddon but overwhelmingly eager to meet it.

The ajar door finally spread wide, framing Raul.

Her breath caught in her throat.

Sleek and powerful, in a summerweight double-breasted
beige business suit, he looked sensationally attractive, supremely poised and shockingly self-assured. Polly lost her
animated colour, ashamed of that helpless flare of physical
response to those dark good looks and that lithe, lean, muscular physique. He was a ruthless and unashamed manipu-
lator.

Black eyes raked over her, black eyes without any shade
of warm gold. Emotionless, businesslike, not even a comforting hint of uncertainty about his stance. 'You look better already,' he remarked levelly.

'I feel better,' Polly was generous enough to admit. 'But
I can't stay here—'

'Of course you can. Where else could you be so well
cared for?'

'I've got something here I want you to explain,' Polly
delivered tautly.

His attention dropped to the envelope clutched between
her tense fingers. 'What is it?'

A shaky little laugh escaped Polly. 'Oh, it's not real
proof of the manipulative lies I was fed...you needn't

worry about that! Your lawyer was far too clever to allow me to retain any original documents, but I took photocopies—'

Raul frowned at her. '*Dios mio*, cut to the base line and tell me what you're talking about,' he incised impatiently. 'You were told no lies at any time!'

'Off the record lies,' Polly extended tightly. 'It was very clever to give me the impression that I was being allowed a reassuring glimpse at highly confidential information.'

Raul angled back his imperious dark head. 'Explain yourself.'

Polly tossed the envelope to the foot of the bed. 'How you can look me in the face and say that I will never know.'

Raul swept up the envelope with an undaunted flourish.

'And don't try to pretend you didn't know about it. When I was asked to sign that contract, I said I couldn't sign until I was given some assurances about the couple who wanted me to act as surrogate for them.'

'The...*couple*?' Raul queried flatly, ebony brows drawing together as he extracted the folded pages from the envelope.

'Your lawyer said that wasn't possible. His clients wanted complete anonymity. So I left. Forty-eight hours later, I got a phone call. I met up in a café with a young bright spark from your lawyer's office. He said he was a clerk,' Polly related jerkily, her resentment and distaste blatant in her strained face as she recalled how easily she had been fooled. 'He said he *understood* my concern about the people who would be adopting my child, and that he was risking his job in allowing me even a glance at such confidential documents—'

'Which confidential documents?' Raul cut in grittily.

'He handed me a profile of that *supposed* couple from an accredited adoption agency. There were no names, no details which might have identified them...' Tears stung Polly's eyes then, her voice beginning to shake with the strength of her feelings. 'And I was really moved by what

I read, by their own personal statements, their complete honesty, their deep longing to have a family. They struck me as wonderful people, and they'd had a h-heartbreaking time struggling to have a child of their own...'

'*Madre mía*...' Raul ground out, half under his breath, scorching golden eyes pinned to her distraught face with mesmeric force.

'And you see,' Polly framed jaggedly, 'I really *liked* that couple. I felt for them, thought they would make terrific parents, would give any child a really loving home...' As a strangled sob swallowed her voice, she crammed a mortified hand against her wobbling mouth and stared in tormented accusation at Raul through swimming blue eyes. 'How *could* you sink that low?' she condemned strickenly.

Raul gazed back at her, strikingly pale now below his olive skin, so still he might have been a stone statue, a stunned light in his piercing dark eyes.

With the greatest difficulty, Polly cleared her throat and breathed unevenly. 'I asked the clerk to let me have an hour reading over that profile and I photocopied it without telling him. That afternoon, I went in and signed the contract. I thought I was doing a really good thing. I thought I would make that couple so happy... I was inexcusably dumb and shortsighted!'

The heavy silence stretched like a rubber band pulled too taut. And then Raul unfroze. In an almost violent gesture, he shook open the pages he still held. He strode over to the window, his broad back turned to her, his tension so pronounced it hummed like a force field in a room that now felt suffocatingly airless.

Polly sank wearily back against the pillows and fought to get a grip on the tears still clogging her aching throat.

Timeless minutes later, Raul swung back, his darkly handsome features grim and forbidding. 'This abhorrent deception was not instigated by me,' he declared, visibly struggling to contain the outrage blazing in his eyes, the revealing rawness to that harshened plea in his own defence. 'I had no knowledge of your request for further information *or* of your initial reluctance to sign that contract.'

'How am I supposed to believe anything you say?'

'Because the guilty party will be called to account,' Raul asserted with wrathful bite. 'At no stage did I give any instruction which might have implied that I would countenance such a deception. There was no need for me to stoop to lies and manipulation. There were other far less scrupulous applicants available—'

'Were there?' Polly breathed, not best pleased to realise that she had featured as one of many.

He was shocked and furious, so furious there was a slight tremor in his fingers as he refolded the pages she had given him. His sincerity was fiercely convincing.

'So now I know why you have no faith in my word. It wasn't only my decision to conceal my identity as the father of your child in Vermont that made you change your mind about fulfilling the contract.'

It was an unfortunate reminder. He only had to mention that cruel masquerade to fill Polly with savage pain and resentment. She surveyed him with angry, bitter eyes. 'I would never, ever have agreed to a single male parent for my child, and when I found out who you really were, I was genuinely appalled—'

Raul skimmed a startled glance at her. '*Dios mio*…"appalled"? What an exaggeration—'

'No exaggeration. I wouldn't give a man with your reputation a pet rabbit to keep, never mind an innocent, helpless baby!' Polly fired back at him.

Raul gazed back at her with complete incredulity. 'What is wrong with my reputation?'

'Read your own publicity,' Polly advised with unconcealed distaste, thinking about the endless string of glamorous women who had been associated with him. There was nothing stable or respectable about Raul's lifestyle.

Outrage sizzled round Raul Zaforteza like an intimidating aura. He snatched in a deep shuddering breath of restraint. 'What right do you have to stand in judgement over me? So subterfuge was employed to persuade you into conceiving my child—I deeply regret that reality, but nothing will alter the situation we're in now. That child you carry is *still* my child!'

Polly turned her head away. 'And mine.'

'The Judgement of Solomon. Are you about to suggest that we divide him or her into two equal halves? Let me tell you now that I will fight to the end to prevent that obnoxious little nerd I met last night raising my child!' Raul delivered with sudden explosive aggression.

Polly blinked. 'What little nerd?'

'Henry Grey informed me that you're engaged to him,' Raul imparted with a feral flash of white teeth. 'And you may believe that that is your business, but *anything* that affects my child's welfare is also very much *my* business now!'

Stunned to realise that Henry should have claimed to be engaged to her, Polly surveyed the volatile male striding up and down the room, like a prowling tiger lashing his tail at the confines of a cage. Why did she want to hold Raul in her arms and soothe him? she asked herself with a sinking heart.

'I think you should leave, Raul.' As that dry voice of reproof cut through the electric atmosphere, Polly tore her mesmerised attention from Raul. In turn, Raul swung round. They both focused in astonishment on the consultant lodged in the doorway.

'*Leave?*' Raul stressed in unconcealed disbelief.

'Only quiet visitors are welcome here,' Rodney Bevan spelt out gravely.

Dressed in an Indian cotton dress the same rich blue as her eyes, Polly turned her face up into the sun and basked, welded to the comfy cushioning on the lounger. The courtyard garden at the centre of the clinic was an enchanting spot on a summer day. Even Henry's unwelcome visit couldn't detract from her pleasure at being surrounded by greenery again.

Henry gave her an accusing look. 'Anybody would think you were enjoying yourself here!'

'It's very restful.'

Until Polly had escaped Henry and his mother for three days, she hadn't appreciated just how wearing their constant badgering had become. She was tired of being pressurised and pushed in a direction she didn't want to go. Now that Raul had found her, she was no longer in hiding. After she had sorted out things with Raul, she would be able to take control of her own life again.

'Mother thinks you should come home,' Henry told her with stiff disapproval.

'You still haven't explained *why* you told Raul we were engaged.'

Henry frowned. 'I should've thought that was obvious. I hoped he'd go away and leave us alone. What's the point of him showing up now? He's just complicating things, swanning up in his flash car and acting like he owns you!'

Strange how even a male as insensitive as Henry had recognised that Raul behaved as if he owned her. Only it wasn't her, it was the baby he believed he owned. Dear heaven, what a mess she was in, Polly conceded worriedly. There was no going back, no way of changing anything. Her baby was also Raul's baby and always would be.

'It was kind of you to call in, Henry,' she murmured quietly. 'Tell your mother that I really appreciate all her kindness, but that I won't be coming back to stay with you—'

'What on earth are you talking about?' Henry had gone all red in the face.

'I just don't want to marry you...I'm sorry.'

'I'll visit later in the week, when you're feeling more yourself.'

As Henry departed, Polly reflected that she was actually

feeling more herself than she had in many weeks. Stepping off the treadmill of exhaustion had given her space to think.

As she slowly, awkwardly raised herself, Raul appeared through a door on the far side of the courtyard. He angled a slashing, searching glance over the little clusters of patients taking the fresh air nearby. Screened by the shrubbery, Polly made no attempt to attract his attention.

His suit was palest grey. He exuded designer chic. In the sunlight, his luxuriant hair gleamed blue-black. His lean, strong face possessed such breathtaking sexy symmetry that her breathing quickened and her sluggish pulses raced. Raul radiated raw sexuality in virile waves. The media said that men thought about sex at least once a minute. One look at Raul was enough to convince her.

But a feeling of stark inadequacy and rejection now threatened her in Raul's radius. How the heck had she ever believed that a male that gorgeous was interested in her? How wilfully blind she had been in Vermont! If a woman excited Raul, he probably pounced on the first date, or maybe he got pounced on, but he had never made a pass at *her*, or even tried to kiss her. At first he had made her as nervous as a cat on hot bricks. But before very long his exquisite manners and flattering interest in her had soothed her inexperienced squirmings in his presence and given her entirely the wrong impression.

Incredibly, she had believed that one of the world's most notorious womanisers was actually a cautious and decent guy, mature enough to want to get to know a woman as a friend before trying to take the relationship any further. Remembering that fact now made Polly feel positively queasy. She had thought Raul was perfect; she had thought he was wonderful; she had thought he was really attracted to her because he continued to seek out her company...

Far from impervious to Raul's cool exasperation when he finally espied her, lurking behind the shrubbery, Polly dropped her head, her shining fall of mahogany hair concealing her taut profile.

'What are you doing out of bed?' Raul demanded the instant he got within hailing distance. 'I'll take you back up to your room.'

'I'm allowed out for fresh air as long as I don't overdo it,' Polly said thinly.

'We'll go inside,' Raul decreed. 'We can't discuss confidential business here.'

Polly swung her legs off the lounger and got up. 'Business? I've learnt the hard way that my baby is not a piece of merchandise.'

'Do you really think I feel any different?' Raul breathed with a raw, bitter edge to his rich, dark drawl. 'Do you really think you're the only one of us to have learnt from this mess?'

She couldn't avoid looking at him in the lift. He stood opposite her, supremely indifferent to the two nurses in the corner studying him with keen female appreciation. He stared at Polly without apology, intense dark eyes welded broodingly to her heart-shaped face and the heated colour steadily building in her cheeks.

She had one question she desperately wanted to ask him. Why did a drop-dead gorgeous heterosexual male of only thirty-one feel the need to hire a surrogate mother to have his child? Why hadn't he just got married? Or, alternatively, why hadn't he simply persuaded one of his innumerable blonde bimbo babes into motherhood? Why surrogacy?

The minute Polly settled herself down on the sofa in her room, Raul breathed with a twist of his expressive mouth, 'You're still angry with me about Vermont. We should deal with that and get it out of the way...it's clouding the real issues at stake here.'

At that statement of intent, Polly stiffened, and her skin prickled with shrinking apprehension. 'Naturally I'm still angry, but I see no point in talking about it. That's in the past now.'

Raul strolled over to the window. He dug a lean brown

hand into the pocket of his well-cut trousers tightening the
fit of the fine fabric over his narrow hips and long, muscular
thighs. Polly found herself abstractedly studying a part of
the male anatomy she had never in her life before studied,
the distinctively manly bulge of his manhood. Flushing to
the roots of her hair, she hurriedly looked away.

But it was so peculiar, she thought bitterly. So peculiar
to be pregnant by a man she had never slept with, never
been intimate with in any way. And Raul Zaforteza was *all*
male, like a walking advertisement for high testosterone
levels and virility. Why on earth had he chosen to have his
child conceived by an anonymous insemination in a doctor's surgery?

'If I'm really honest, I wanted to meet you and talk to
you right from the moment you signed the contract,' Raul
drawled tautly, interrupting her seething thoughts.

'Why, for heaven's sake?'

'I knew my child would want to know what you were
really like.'

A cold chill of repulsion trickled down Polly's spine. So
impersonal, so practical, so utterly unfeeling a motivation.

'After your mother died, I was aware that you were in
considerable distress,' Raul continued levelly. 'You needed
support...who *else* was there to provide that support? If
you hadn't discovered that I was the baby's father, you
wouldn't have been so upset. And isn't it time you told me
how you *did* penetrate that secret?'

In her mind's eye, Polly pictured Soledad and all the
numerous members of her equally dependent family being
flung off the ancestral ranch the older woman had described
in Venezuela. She gulped. 'You gave yourself away. Your
behaviour...well, it made me suspicious. I worked the truth
out for myself,' she lied stiltedly.

'You're a liar...Soledad told you,' Raul traded without
skipping a beat, shrewd dark eyes grimly amused by her
startled reaction. 'A major oversight on my part. Two

women stuck all those weeks in the same house? The barriers came down and you became friendly—'

'Soledad would never have betrayed you if you hadn't come into my life without admitting who you were!' Polly interrupted defensively. 'She couldn't cope with being forced to pretend that she didn't know you.'

'I was at fault there,' Raul acknowledged openly, honestly, taking her by surprise. 'I'm aware of that now. Vermont *was* a mistake...it personalised what should have remained impersonal and compromised my sense of honour.'

A mistake? A gracious admission of fault, an apology underwritten. Gulping back a spurt of angry revealing words, Polly swallowed hard. He was so smooth, so reasonable and controlled. She wanted to scratch her nails down the starkly handsome planes of those high cheekbones to make him feel for even one *second* something of what she had suffered!

'So, now that you know how I found out, are Soledad and her family still working for you?' Polly enquired stiffly.

Raul dealt her a wry smile. 'Her family is, but Soledad has moved to Caracas to look after her grandchildren while her daughter's at work.'

A light knock at the door announced the entry of a maid, bearing Polly's afternoon tea. Raul asked for black coffee, it not occurring to him for one moment that as a visitor he might not be entitled to refreshment. Blushing furiously, the maid literally rushed to satisfy his request.

Cradling the coffee elegantly in one lean hand, Raul sank down lithely into the armchair opposite her. 'Are you comfortable here?'

'Very.'

'But obviously it's a challenge to fill the empty hours. I'll get a video recorder sent in, some tapes, books...I know what you like,' Raul asserted with complete confidence. 'I should've thought of it before.'

'I'm not happy with what this place must be costing

you,' Polly told him in a sudden rush. 'Especially as I am not going to honour that contract.'

Raul scanned her anxious blue eyes. A slight smile momentarily curved his wide, sensual mouth. 'You need some time and space to consider that decision. Right now, I have no intention of putting pressure on you—'

'Just having you in the same room is pressure,' Polly countered uncomfortably. 'Having you pay my bills makes it even worse.'

'Whatever happens, I'm still the father of your baby. That makes you my responsibility.'

'The softly, softly, catchee monkey routine won't work with me... I'm so fed up with people telling me that I don't know what I want, or that I don't know what I'm doing.' Polly raised her small head high and valiantly clashed with brilliant black eyes as sharp as paint. 'The truth is that I've grown up a lot in the last few months...'

Raul held up a fluid and silencing hand in a gesture that came so naturally to him that she instinctively closed her lips. 'In swift succession over the past year or so you have lost the three people you cared about most in this world. Your father, your mother and your godmother. That is bound to be affecting your judgement *and* your view of the future. All I want to do is give you another possible view.'

Setting aside his empty coffee cup, he rose gracefully upright again. Polly watched him nervously, the tip of her tongue stealing out to moisten the dry curve of her lower lip.

Raul's attention dropped to the soft, generous pink curve of her mouth and lingered, and she felt the oddest buzzing current in the air, her slight frame automatically tensing in reaction. Raul stiffened, the dark rise of blood emphasising the slashing line of his hard cheekbones. Swinging on his heel, he strode over to the window and pushed it wider.

'It's stuffy in here... As I was saying, an alternative view of the future,' he continued flatly. 'You can't possibly *want* to marry that little jerk Henry Grey—'

Taken aback, Polly sat up straighter. 'How do you know?'

His chiselled profile clenched into aggressive lines. 'He's just being greedy...he wouldn't look twice at a woman expecting another man's child *unless* she was an heiress!'

Polly flinched at that revealing assertion. 'So you found out about my godmother's will...'

'Naturally...' Raul skimmed an assured glance in her direction. 'And the good news is that you don't have to marry Henry to inherit that money and make a new start. You're only twenty-one; you have your whole life in front of you. Why clog it up with Henry? He's a pompous bore. I'm prepared to *give* you that million pounds to dump him!'

In sheer shock, Polly's lips fell open. She began to rise off the sofa. 'I b-beg your pardon?' she stammered shakily, convinced he couldn't possibly have said what she thought he had said.

Raul swung fluidly round to face her again. 'You heard me. Forget that stupid will, and for the present forget the baby too...just ditch that loser!'

Her blue eyes opened very wide. She gaped at him, and then she took a step forward, fierce anger leaping up inside her. 'How dare you try to bribe me into doing what *you* want me to do? How *dare* you do that?'

Raul's cool façade cracked to reveal the cold anger beneath. He sent her a sizzling look of derision. '*Caramba!* Surely you'd prefer to stay rich and single when Henry's the only option on offer?'

Without an instant of hesitation, Polly snatched up the water jug by the bed with a feverish hand and slung the contents at him. '*That's* what I think of your filthy offer! I'm not for sale this time and I never will be again!'

Soaked by that sizeable flood, and astonished by both her attack and that outburst, Raul stood there dripping and downright incredulous. As his lean fingers raked his wet hair off his brow, his dark eyes flamed to a savage golden blaze.

'I'm not sorry,' Polly admitted starkly.

Raul slung her a searing look of scantily leashed fury. *'Por Dios*…I am leaving before I say or do something I might regret!' he bit out rawly.

The door snapped shut in his imperious wake. Polly snatched in a slow steadying breath and realised that even her hands were shaking. She had never met with a temper that hot before.

# CHAPTER THREE

A VIDEO recorder arrived, complete with a whole collection of tapes, and was installed in Polly's room by lunchtime the following day.

As a gesture, it was calculated to make her feel guilty. That evening, Polly sat in floods of tears just picking through titles like *The Quiet Man* and *Pretty Woman* and *Sabrina*. All escapist romantic movies, picked by a male who knew her tastes far too well for comfort. She grabbed up another tissue in despair.

Raul Zaforteza unleashed a temper she hadn't known she had. He filled her to overflowing with violent, resentful and distressingly confused emotions. She hated him, she told herself fiercely. He was tearing her apart. She hated him even more when she felt herself react to the humiliating pull of his magnetic sexual attraction.

Worse, Raul understood her so much better than she understood him. In Vermont, she had trustingly revealed too many private thoughts and feelings, while he had been coolly evaluating her, like a scientist studying something curious under a microscope. Why? He had answered that straight off the top of his head and without hesitation.

*So that he could answer her child's questions about her in the future.*

Polly shivered at the memory of that admission, chilled to the marrow and hurt beyond belief. It wasn't possible to get more detached than that from another human being. But how many times had Raul already emphasised that there was nothing but that hateful surrogate contract between them? And why was she still torturing herself with that reality?

He had coolly, contemptuously offered her a million
pounds to dump Henry and stay single. And why had he
done that? Simply because he felt threatened by the idea of
her marrying. Why hadn't she grasped that fact sooner? If
she married, Raul would be forced, whether he liked it or
not, to stand back while another man raised his child. So
why hadn't she told him she wasn't planning to marry
Henry?

Polly was honest with herself on that point. She hadn't
seen *why* she should tell him the truth. What business was
it of his? And she had been prepared to hide behind a pretend engagement to Henry, a face-saving pretence that suggested her life had moved on since Vermont. Only Raul
had destroyed that pretence. Acquainted as he was with the
intricacies of her godmother's will, he had realised that that
inheritance was the only reason Henry was willing to marry
her. It mortified Polly that Raul should have guessed even
that. In his presence, she was beginning to feel as if she
was being speedily stripped of every defence.

But then what did she know about men? It was laughable
to be so close to the birth of her own child and still be so
ignorant. But her father had been a strict, puritanical man,
whose rules and restrictions had made it impossible for her
to enjoy a normal social life. It had even been difficult to
hang onto female friends with a father who invariably of-
fended them by criticising their clothing or their behaviour.

She had had a crush on a boy in her teens, but he had
quickly lost interest when her father refused to allow her
to go out with him. When she had started the university
degree course that she'd never got to finish, she had lived
so close to the campus she had had to continue living at
home. She had kept house for her father, assisted in his
many church activities and, when his stationery business
began to fail, helped with his office work.

She had sneaked out to the occasional party. Riven with
guilt at having lied to get out, she had endured a few over-
enthusiastic clinches, wondering what all the fuss was about

while she pushed away groping, over-familiar hands, unable to comprehend why any sane female would want to respond to such crude demands.

She had met another boy while studying. Like his predecessors, he had been unwilling to come to the house and meet her father just to get permission to take her out at night. At first he had thought it was a bit of laugh to see her only during the day. Then one lunchtime he had taken her back to his flat and tried to get her to go to bed with him. She had said no. He had ditched her there and then, called her 'a pathetic, boring little virgin' and soon replaced her with a more available girl who didn't expect love and commitment in return for sex.

It had taken Raul Zaforteza to teach Polly what she had never felt before...a deep, dark craving for physical contact as tormenting to endure as a desperate thirst...

Polly was restless that evening. Aware that she wasn't asleep, one of the nurses brought her in a cup of tea at ten, and thoughtfully lent her a magazine to read.

As always, during the night, her door was kept ajar to allow the staff to check easily and quietly on her. So when, out of the corner of her eye, Polly saw the door open wider, she turned with a smile for the nurse she was expecting to see and then froze in surprise when she saw Raul instead. Visiting time finished at nine, and it was now after eleven.

'How did you get in?' Polly asked in a startled whisper.

Raul leant lithely back against the door until it snapped softly shut. In a black dinner jacket and narrow black trousers, a bow tie at his throat, he exuded sophisticated cool. 'Talked my way past the security guard and chatted up the night sister.'

Strolling forward, he set a tub of ice cream in front of her. 'Peppermint—your favourite...my peace offering,' he murmured with a lazy smile.

That charismatic smile hit Polly like a shot of adrenalin in her veins. Every trace of drowsiness evaporated. Her

heart jumped, her mouth ran dry and burning colour started
to creep up her throat. He lifted the teaspoon from the cup
and saucer on the bed-table she had pushed away and settled it down helpfully on top of the tub.

'Eat it before it melts,' he advised, settling down on the
end of the bed in an indolent sprawl.

It shook her that Raul should recall that peppermint was
her favorite flavour. It shook her even more that he should
take the trouble to call in with ice cream at this hour of the
night when he had obviously been out somewhere.

With a not quite steady hand, Polly removed the lid on
the tub. 'Henry lied,' she confided abruptly. 'We're not
engaged. I'm not going to marry him.'

In the intimate pool of light shed by the Anglepoise lamp
by the bed, a wolfish grin slashed Raul's darkly handsome
features. Polly was so mesmerised by it, she dug her teaspoon into empty air instead of the tub and only discovered
the ice cream by touch.

'You could do a lot better than him, *cielita*,' he responded softly.

Polly's natural sense of fairness prompted her to add,
'Henry isn't that bad. He was honest. It wasn't like he
pretended to fancy me or anything like that...'

Slumberous dark eyes semi-screened by lush ebony
lashes, Raul emitted a low-pitched laugh that sent an odd
little tremor down her sensitive spine. 'Henry has no taste.'

The silence that fell seemed to hum in her eardrums.

Feeling that languorous heaviness in her breasts, the
surge of physical awareness she dreaded, Polly shifted uneasily and leapt straight back into speech. 'Why did you
decide to hire a surrogate?' she asked baldly. 'It doesn't
make sense to me.'

His strong face tensed. 'I wanted to have a child while
I was still young enough to play with a child...'

'And the right woman just didn't come along?' Polly
assumed as the silence stretched.

'Perhaps I should say that I like women but I like my

freedom better. Let's leave it at that,' Raul suggested smoothly.

'I'm so sorry I signed that contract.' Troubled eyes blue as violets rested on him, her heart-shaped face strained. 'I don't know how I thought I could actually go through with it...but at the time I suppose I couldn't think of anything but how sick my mother was.'

'I should never have picked you. The psychologist said that he wasn't convinced you understood how hard it would be to surrender your child—'

'Did he?'

'He said you were too intense, too idealistic.'

Polly frowned. 'So why was I chosen?'

Raul lifted a broad shoulder in a slight fatalistic shrug that was very Latin. 'I *liked* you. I didn't want to have a baby with a woman I couldn't even like.'

'I was a really bad choice,' Polly muttered ruefully. 'Now I wish you'd listened to the psychologist.'

Raul vented a rather grim laugh. 'I never listen to what I don't want to hear. People who work for me know that, and they like to please me. That's why you were fed lies to persuade you into signing the contract. A very junior lawyer got smart and set you up. He didn't tell his boss what he'd done until *after* you'd signed. He expected an accolade for his ingenuity but instead he got fired.'

'Did he?' Polly showed her surprise.

'*Sí...*' Raul's mouth tightened. 'But my lawyer saw no reason to tell me what had happened. He had no idea that either of us would ever be in a position to find out.'

Polly ate the ice cream, lashes lowering as she savoured each cool, delicious spoonful. The seconds ticked by. Raul watched her. She was aware of his intent scrutiny, curiously satisfied by the attention, but extremely nervous of it too, as if she was a mouse with a hawk circling overhead. It was so quiet, so very quiet at that hour of the night, no distant buzzing bells, no quick-moving feet in the corridor outside.

And then Polly stiffened, a muffled little sound of discomfort escaping her as the baby chose that moment to give her an athletic kick.

Raul leant forward. '*Que*...what is it?' he demanded anxiously.

'The baby. It's always liveliest at night.' She met the question in his eyes and flushed, reaching a sudden decision. Setting down the ice cream, she pushed the bedding back the few necessary inches, knowing that she was perfectly decently covered in her cotton nightie but still feeling horrendously shy.

Raul drew closer and rested his palm very lightly on her stomach. As he felt the movement beneath his fingers, a look of wonder filled his dark, shimmering gaze and he smiled with sudden quick brilliance. 'That's amazing,' he breathed. 'Do you know if it's a boy or a girl yet?'

'Mr Bevan offered to tell me but I didn't want to know,' Polly admitted unevenly, deeply unsettled by that instant of intimate sharing but undeniably touched by his fascination. 'I like surprises better.'

Raul slowly removed his palm and tugged the sheet back into place. His hands weren't quite steady. Noting that, she wondered why. She could still feel the cool touch of his hand like a burning imprint on her own flesh. He was so close she could hardly breathe, her own awareness of him so pronounced it was impossible to fight. At best, she knew she could only hope to conceal her reaction, but though she was desperate to think of something to say to distract him her mind was suddenly a blank.

'You can be incredibly sweet...' Raul remarked, half under his breath.

Her intent gaze roamed over him, lingering helplessly on the glossy luxuriance of his black hair, the hard, clean line of his high cheekbones and the dark roughening of his jawline that suggested a need to shave twice a day. Reaching the wide, passionate curve of his mouth, she wondered as she had wondered so often before what he tasted like. Then, wildly flustered by that disturbing thought, her eyes lifted, full of confusion, and the dark golden lure of his gaze entrapped and held her in thrall.

'And incredibly tempting,' Raul confided huskily as he brought his sensual mouth very slowly down on hers.

She could have pulled back with ease; he gave her every opportunity. But at the first touch of his lips on hers she dissolved into a hot, melting pool of acquiescence. With a muffled groan, he closed his hand into the tumbling fall of her hair to steady himself and let his tongue stab deep into the tender interior of her mouth. And the whole tenor of the kiss changed.

Excitement so intense it burned flamed instantly through her, bringing her alive with a sudden shocking vitality that made her screamingly aware of every inch of her own humming body. And as soon as it began she ached for more, lacing desperate fingers into the silky thickness of his hair, palms sliding down then to curve over to his cheekbones. Only at some dim, distant, uncaring level was she conscious of the buzzing, irritating sound somewhere close by.

Raul released her with a stifled expletive in Spanish and sprang off the bed. With dazed eyes, Polly watched him pull out a mobile phone. And in the deep silence she heard the high-pitched vibration of a woman's voice before he put the phone to his ear.

'*Dios*...I'll be down in a moment,' Raul murmured curtly, and, switching the phone off, he dug it back into his pocket.

'I'm sorry but I have to go. I have someone waiting in the car.' He raked restive fingers through his now thoroughly tousled black hair, glittering golden eyes screened from her searching scrutiny, mouth compressed into a ferocious line. 'I'll see you soon. *Buenas noches*.'

The instant he left the room, Polly thrust back the bedding and scrambled awkwardly out of bed. She flew over to the window which overlooked the front entrance and pulled back the curtain. She saw the limo...and she saw the beautiful blonde in her sleek, short crimson dress pacing beside it. Then she watched the blonde arrange herself in a studied pose against the side of the luxury car so that she looked like a glamorous model at an automobile show.

Polly rushed back across the room to douse the lamp and then returned to the window. Raul emerged from the clinic. The blonde threw herself exuberantly into his arms. Polly's nerveless fingers dropped from the curtain. She reeled back against the cold wall and closed her arms round her trembling body, feeling sick and dizzy and utterly disgusted with herself.

Oh, dear heaven, why hadn't she slapped his face for him? Why, oh, why had she allowed him to kiss her? Feeling horribly humiliated and raw, she got back into bed with none of the adrenalin-charged speed with which she had vacated it. Tonight Raul had been out with his latest blonde. Now they were either moving on to some nightclub or heading for a far more intimate setting. She could barely credit that Raul had called in to see her in the middle of a date with another woman, as relaxed and unhurried as if he'd had all the time in the world to spend with her.

Polly felt murderous. She could still see the ice cream tub glimmering in the darkness. Gosh, weren't you a pushover? a sarcastic little inner voice gibed. Easily impressed, pitifully vulnerable. Her defences hadn't stood a chance with Raul in a more approachable mood. And he hadn't even kissed her because he was attracted to her—oh, no. Nothing so simple and nothing less flattering than the true explanation she suspected.

He had felt the baby move. That had been a disturbingly intimate and emotional experience for them both. For the first time they had crossed the barriers of that contract and actually *shared* something that related to the baby. And Raul was a very physical male who had, in the heat of the moment, reacted in an inappropriately physical way. The constraint of his abrupt departure had revealed his unease with that development. She was convinced he wouldn't ever let anything like that happen between them again.

Yet for so long Polly had ached for Raul to kiss her, and that passionate kiss had outmatched her every naive expectation. Without ever touching her, Raul had taught her to crave him like a dangerous drug. Now she despised herself and felt all the shame of her own wantonly eager response. She did hate him now, she told herself vehemently. Technically she might still be a virgin, but she wasn't such an idiot that she didn't know that sexual feelings could both tempt and confuse. Her response had had nothing to do with love or intelligence.

She had stopped loving Raul the same day that she'd discovered how he had been deceiving her in Vermont. But the complexity of their current relationship was plunging her into increasing turmoil. For what relationship *did* they have? She wasn't his lover but she was expecting his baby, and she couldn't even claim that they were friends, could she...?

A magnificent floral arrangement arrived from Raul the next day. Polly asked the maid to pass it on to one of the other patients. She didn't want to be reminded of Raul every time she looked across the room.

He phoned in the afternoon. 'How are you?'

'Turning somersaults,' Polly said brittly. 'Leafing through my frantically crammed social diary to see what I'll be doing today. Do I really need to stay here much longer?'

'Rod thinks so,' Raul reminded her. 'Look, I'll be away on business for the next week. I wanted to leave a contact number with you so that you can get in touch if you need to.'

'I can't imagine there being any need when I'm surrounded by medical staff and being waited on hand and foot.'

'OK. I'll phone *you*—'

Polly breathed in deep. 'Would you mind if I asked you not to?'

'I don't like having this type of conversation on the phone. It's a very female method of warfare,' Raul drawled grimly.

'I was just asking for a little space,' Polly countered tightly. 'In the circumstances, I don't think that's unreasonable. You may be the father of my child, but we don't have a personal relationship.'

'I'll see you when I get back from Paris, Polly.'

The line went dead. But Polly continued to grip the receiver frantically tight. She didn't want to see him; she didn't want to hear from him. Her eyes smarted. But the tears were nothing to do with him. Late on in pregnancy women were often more emotional and tearful, she reminded herself staunchly.

Mid-morning, late in the following week, Polly had just put on a loose red jersey dress with a V-neckline and short sleeves when Raul arrived to visit her. Hearing the knock on the door of her room, she emerged from the bathroom, still struggling to brush her long hair. She fell still in an awkward pose when she realised who it was.

Her heart skipped a complete beat. Raul was wearing a navy pinstriped business suit so sharply tailored it fitted his magnificent physique like a glove. Worn with a dark blue shirt and red silk tie, it made him look sensationally attractive and dynamic. Her throat closed over. It felt like a hundred years since she had last seen him. She wanted to move closer, had to forcefully still her feet where she stood.

Raul strolled forward and casually reached up to pluck the brush from her loosened hold. Gently turning her round by her shoulders, he teased loose the tangle she had been fighting with before returning the brush to her hand. 'I owe you an apology for my behaviour on my last visit,' he murmured with conviction.

Polly tensed. There was a mirror on the back of the bathroom door. She could see his reflection, the cool gravity of his expression, the dark brilliance of his assessing gaze.

Colour stained Polly's cheeks but she managed to laugh. 'For goodness' sake,' she said with determined lightness, 'there's no need for an apology. It was just a kiss…no big deal!'

Something bright flared in his dark eyes and then they were veiled, his sensual mouth curling slightly. '*Bueno*. I wondered if you would like to have lunch out today?'

In surprise, Polly swivelled round, all constraint put to flight by that unexpected but very welcome suggestion that she might return to the outside world for a few hours. 'I'd love to!'

In the foyer they ran into Janice Grey.

'Oh, dear, were you coming to visit me?' Polly muttered with a dismay made all the more pungent by a guilty sense of relief. 'I'm so sorry. I'm afraid we're going out for lunch.'

'That does surprise me.' Janice raised an enquiring brow. 'I understood you were here to rest.'

'I'm under the strictest instructions to see that she doesn't overtire herself, Mrs Grey,' Raul interposed with a coolly pleasant smile. 'I'm also grateful to have the opportunity to thank you for all the support you have given Polly in recent weeks.'

The middle-aged blonde gave him a thin smile and turned to Polly. 'Henry said that you weren't coming back to stay with us.' She then shot Raul an arch look that didn't conceal her hostility. 'Do I hear wedding bells in the air?'

Polly paled, and then hot, mortified colour flooded her cheeks. The silence simmered.

Raul stepped calmly into the breach. 'I'm sure Polly will keep you in touch with events, Mrs Grey.

'A tough cookie,' Raul remarked of the older woman as he settled Polly into the limousine a few minutes later. 'I'm relieved that you didn't choose to confide in her about our legal agreement. But why the hell did you look so uncomfortable?'

Polly thought of those crazy weeks in Vermont, when she had foolishly allowed herself to be wildly, recklessly in love with Raul. Her imagination had known no limits when every moment she could she'd tried to forget the fact that she was pregnant. Those stupid girlish daydreams about marrying Raul were now a severe embarrassment to recall. She had to think fast to come up with another explanation for her discomfiture.

'Janice *was* kind to me...but she'd never have offered me a room if she hadn't known about my inheritance. She couldn't understand why I wasn't prepared to marry Henry for the sake of that money. She thought I was being very foolish and shortsighted.'

'You don't need to make a choice like that now. In any case, *gatita*...you're far too young to be thinking about marriage.'

An awkward little silence fell. Polly was very tense. She was already scolding herself for having reacted to Raul's invitation as if his only aim was to give her a pleasant outing. Raul did nothing without good reason. Over lunch, Raul was undoubtedly planning to open a serious discussion about their baby's future. The subject could not be avoided any longer, and this time she would try to be as calm and rational as possible.

'Waiting to hear what you're going to say makes me very nervous,' she nonetheless heard herself confide abruptly. 'I may be pregnant, but I'm not likely to pop off at the first piece of bad news. Do you think you could just tell me right now up front whether or not you're planning to take me to court after the baby's born?'

Raul sent her a shimmering glance, his mouth curling. 'Much good it would do me if I did have such plans. Although it seems very wrong to me, in this country I have no legal rights as the father of your child.'

'*Honestly?*' Polly surveyed him through very wide and surprised blue eyes. 'But what about the contract?'

'Forget the contract. It might as well not exist now. Do you seriously think that I would even want to take such a personal and private matter into a courtroom?'

'I never thought of that,' Polly admitted, suddenly feeling quite weak with the strength of her relief. 'I just had nightmares about being extradited to the USA.'

An involuntary smile briefly curved Raul's lips. 'Force wouldn't work in a situation like this.'

Did he think that persuasion would? Polly worried about that idea. She knew that her own convictions ran so deep and strong he had no hope of changing her mind; she was determined to keep her baby. But she was burdened by the increasingly guilty awareness that that wasn't very fair to Raul, and that some way, somehow, they had to find a compromise that would be bearable for them both.

Yet where could they possibly find that compromise? Raul had chosen surrogacy because he wanted a child, but not a child he had to share in a conventional relationship. Raul had opted for a detached, businesslike arrangement without strings. But no matter what happened now he had no hope of acquiring sole custody of his own child. How could she not feel guilty about that?

Raul took her back to a luxury apartment in Mayfair. Polly felt intimidated by the grandeur of her surroundings. A light and exquisitely cooked lunch was served by a quiet and unobtrusive manservant. Throughout the meal, Raul chatted about his business trip to Paris. He was very entertaining, a sophisticated and amusing raconteur. But, while she laughed and smiled in response, all she could really think about was how easily he had fooled her with that charismatic polish in Vermont.

It meant nothing. It just meant he had terrific social skills. She had learned to read Raul well enough to recognise that essential detachment just beneath the surface, not to mention his smooth ability to avoid giving personal information. All those visits in Vermont and what had she picked up about him? That he had no close family alive, that he was a businessman who travelled a lot, and that he had been born in Venezuela. Precious little.

Raul ran hooded dark eyes over her abstracted face. 'I feel like you're not with me.'

'Perhaps I'm tired,' she said uncomfortably.

Instantly Raul thrust back his chair and rose lithely upright. 'Then you should lie down in one of the guest rooms for a while.'

'No...we need to talk,' Polly acknowledged tautly. 'I want to get that over with.'

Leaving the table, she settled down into a comfortable armchair. The coffee was served. Raul paced restively over to the window and then gazed across the room at her. 'Don't look so anxious...it makes me feel like a bully,' he admitted grimly.

Polly clutched her cup. 'You're not that,' she acknowledged fairly. 'You've been very patient and more understanding than I could ever have expected.'

Raul spread lean brown hands with an eloquence that never failed to engage her attention. 'I have a possible solution to this situation. Please hear me out,' he urged.

Tense as a bowstring, Polly sat very still.

'The biggest difference between us is that I planned to be a parent from the very outset of our association,' Raul delineated with measured clarity. 'But *you* did not. When you became pregnant you did not expect to take on permanent responsibility for that child.'

Polly nodded in wary, reluctant agreement.

'I think you're too young to handle becoming a single parent. I understand that you have become attached to the baby, and that you are naturally very concerned about its future well-being. But if you choose to keep the baby you will have to sacrifice the freedom that most young women of your age take for granted.'

Polly gave him a stubborn look. 'I know that. I'm not

stupid. And I'm hardly likely to miss what I've never had—'

'But you *could* have that freedom now. You should be making plans to return to university to complete your degree,' Raul told her steadily. 'If you let me take my child back to Venezuela, I will allow you access visits, regular reports, photographs. I will agree to any reasonable request. My child will know you as his mother but you will not be the primary carer.'

Raul had taken her very much by surprise. Polly hadn't expected such a willingness to compromise from a male to whom she sensed 'compromise' was an unfamiliar word. On his terms, she guessed it was a very generous offer. He was offering to share their child to some extent, and that was a lot more than she had anticipated.

'I believe every child deserves two parents,' she responded awkwardly. 'Two parents on the spot.'

'That's impossible.'

'I was brought up by my father, and there wasn't a day I didn't long for my mother.'

'This child may be a boy.'

'I don't think that makes any difference. Because of my own experiences, I couldn't face being parted from my child. Whatever it takes, I need to *be* there for my baby and do the very best I can to be a good mother.' Polly was very tense as she struggled to verbalise her own deepest feelings. 'And, yes, it is a very great pity that I didn't work that out before I signed that contract…but my only excuse is that I honestly didn't even begin to understand how I would feel once I was actually pregnant.'

'That's in the past now. We need to concentrate on the present.' With that rather deflating assurance, Raul flung back his darkly handsome head, his dark eyes formidable in their penetration. 'If you really mean what you say when you protest that you intend to be the very best mother you can be…then you must move to Venezuela.'

'*Venezuela?*' Polly exclaimed, wildly disconcerted at

having that stunning suggestion flung at her in cool challenge.

'I will set you up in a house there. You will have every comfort and convenience, and your child as well.'

Polly blinked, still attempting to absorb a staggering proposition that entailed moving to the other side of the world. 'I *couldn't*—'

'*Por Dios*…ask yourself if you are being fair. If the child needs his mother, then he also needs his father. And that child will inherit everything I possess.' Raul spelt out that reminder with imperious pride and impatience.

'Money isn't everything, Raul—'

'Don't be facile. I'm talking about a way of life that you have not the slightest conception of,' Raul returned very drily, watching her flush. 'At least be practical, Polly. My child needs to know that Venezuelan heritage, the language, the people, the culture. If you won't come to Venezuela, what am I to do? With the claims on my time, I can't possibly visit the UK often enough to form a close relationship with my child.'

Polly tried to picture living in Venezuela, with Raul picking up all her bills, walking in and out of her life with one blonde babe girlfriend after another and eventually taking a wife. No matter how he might feel now, she was convinced that he would succumb to matrimony sooner or later. In such a situation she would always be an outsider, an interloper, neither family nor friend, and a lot of people would simply assume that she was his discarded mistress. She knew she would never be able to cope with such a dependent, humiliating existence on the fringe of Raul's world. She needed to get on with her own life. It was time to be honest about that reality.

'Raul…I want to stay in the UK with my baby. I don't want to live in Venezuela, having you oversee every move I make,' Polly admitted, watching him bridle in apparent disbelief at that statement. 'You have the right to be involved in your child's future…but what you seem to forget is that that future is *my* life as well! Anyway, you may not think it now, but some day you'll get married, have other children—'

Raul released his breath in a charged hiss of frustration. 'I would sooner be dead than married!'

'But you see...I *don't* feel the same way,' Polly shared with rueful honesty. 'I would like to think that even as an unmarried mum I will get married eventually.'

'Saying that to me is the equivalent of blackmail, Polly,' Raul condemned, pale with anger beneath his golden skin, eyes hot as sunlight in that lean, dark, devastating face. 'I do not want *any* other man involved in my child's upbringing!'

Temper stirred in Polly, and the more she thought about that blunt and unashamed declaration the angrier she became. Did Raul really believe that he had the right to demand that she live like a nun for the next twenty years? Lonely, unloved, celibate. She stared at him. Yes, that was what he believed and what he wanted, if he was not to have sole custody of their child.

Raising herself out of the armchair, Polly straightened her slight shoulders and stood up. 'You are so *incredibly* selfish and spoilt!' she accused fiercely.

Astonished by that sudden indictment, Raul strode across the room, closing the distance between them. 'I can't believe that you can dare to say that to me—'

'I expect not...as you've already told me, you're accustomed to people who want to please you, who are eager to tell you only what you want to hear!' Polly shot back with unconcealed scorn. 'Well, I'm *not* one of those people!'

His eyes blazed. 'I have bent over backwards to be fair—'

'At what *personal* sacrifice and inconvenience?' Polly slung back, trembling with rage. 'You are a playboy with a reputation as a womaniser. You enjoy your freedom, don't you?'

'Why shouldn't I?' Raul was unmoved by that angle of

attack. 'I don't lie to the women who pass through my life. I don't promise true love or permanency—'

'Because you've never *had* to, have you? You know, listening to you, Raul…I despise my own sex. But I despise you most of all,' Polly confessed, with hands knotting into furious fists by her side. 'It's one rule for you and another for me—a hypocritical sexist double standard the belongs in the Prehistoric ages with Neanderthals like you! You say you want this child, but you didn't want a child badly enough to make a commitment like other men, did you? And what do you offer me—?'

'The only two possible remedies to the mess we're now in. I'm not about to apologise because you do not like the imperfect sound of reality,' Raul delivered with slashing bite.

'Reality? You call it "reality" to offer me a choice between giving up my child almost completely…and living like a *nun* in Venezuela?'

Raul flicked her a grimly amused glance. 'You want the licence to sleep around?'

'You know very well that's not what I'm trying to say!'

'But you wouldn't want me to share your bed without all that idealistic love, commitment and permanency jazz…would you, *querida*?' Raul breathed with sizzling golden eyes, watching her freeze in shock at that plunge into the more intimate and personal. 'You see, what you want and what I want we can't have, because we both want something different!'

Every scrap of colour drained from Polly's face. 'I *don't* want you…like that,' she framed jerkily.

Raul cast her a glittering appraisal that was all male and all-knowing. 'Oh, yes, you do…that sexual hunger has been there between us from the moment we met.'

Polly backed away from him. She could not cope with having his knowledge of her attraction to him thrown in her teeth. 'No—'

'I didn't take advantage of you because I knew it would end in your tears.'

'Don't kid yourself…I might've ditched you first!' Polly told him with very real loathing, her pride so wounded she wanted to kill him. 'And let me tell you something else too, I put a much higher price on myself than your interchangeable blonde babes do.'

'I admire that…I really do,' Raul incised with complete cool, his temper back under wraps again at disorientating, galling speed. 'You have such rigid moral values, *gatita*. Well, warned in advance, I was careful to keep my distance in Vermont.'

Polly shuddered with a rage that was out of control, a rage that had its roots in pain and violent resentment. She was shattered by the sudden ripping down of the careful barriers that had made it possible for them to skim along the surface of their complex relationship. Without those barriers, and shorn by Raul of all face-saving defences, she was flailing wildly.

A look of positive loathing written in her furious eyes, she snapped, 'Then you'll have no problem understanding that the only way you'll ever get me to Venezuela…the only way you'll *ever* achieve full custody of your child…is to marry me, Raul!'

A silence fell between them like a giant black hole, waiting to entrap the unwary.

Raul was now formidably still, brilliant dark eyes icy with incredulity. 'That's not funny, Polly. Take it back.'

'Why? Do you want me to lie to you? Say I didn't mean it?' Polly demanded rawly as she tipped her head back, mahogany hair rippling back from her furiously flushed face. 'I'm being honest with you. If I stay here in the UK, I will get on with my life and you will *not* interfere with that life! I am not prepared to go to Venezuela as anything *other* than a wife!'

Raul sent her a derisive look that said he was unimpressed. 'You are not serious.'

Polly studied him with so much bitterness inside her she marvelled she didn't explode like a destructive weapon. 'I am. Let's see how good you are at making sacrifices when you expect *me* to sacrifice everything! Why? Because I'm not rich and powerful like you? Or because I'm going to be the mother of your child and you have this weird idea that a decent mother has no entitlement to any life of her own?'

Raul jerked as if she had struck him, a feverish flush slowly darkening his hard cheekbones.

This time the silence that fell screamed with menace.

A tiny pulse flickered at the whitened edge of his fiercely compressed mouth. His hands had closed into fists, betraying his struggle for self-command. But, most frightening of all for Polly, for the very first time Raul stared back at her with very real hatred. Cold, hard, deadly loathing. And, in shock, Polly fell silent, mind turning blank, all the fight and anger draining from her, leaving only fear in their place.

'I'll take you back to the clinic,' Raul drawled with raw finality. 'There is no point in allowing this offensive dialogue to continue.'

# CHAPTER FOUR

Two days later, Polly was still recovering from the effects of that catastrophic lunch out.

But her mind was briefly removed from her own problems when she picked up a magazine dated from the previous month and learnt that her childhood friend, Maxie Kendall, had got married, indeed had already been married for several weeks. Maxie and her husband, Angelos Petronides, had kept their marriage a secret until they were ready to make a public announcement. Polly read the article and scrutinised the photos with great interest, and a pleased smile on Maxie's behalf.

She had last met Maxie at the reading of Nancy Leeward's will. Her godmother had actually had three goddaughters, Polly and Maxie and Darcy. Although the girls had been close friends well into their teens, their adult lives had taken them in very different directions.

Maxie had become a famous model, with a tangled love life in London. Darcy had been a single parent, who rarely left her home in Cornwall. Polly had tried to keep in touch with both women but regular contact had gradually lapsed, not least because Darcy and Maxie were no longer friends.

'Isn't she gorgeous?' one of the nurses groaned in admiration, looking over her shoulder at the main picture of Maxie on the catwalk. 'I would give my eye teeth to look like that!'

'Who wouldn't?' Polly's smile of amused agreement slid away as she found herself reflecting that Maxie closely resembled what appeared to be Raul's ideal of a sexually attractive woman. Tall, blonde and stunning. And here she was, a five-foot-one-inch-tall, slightly built brunette, who had never looked glamorous in her life.

She grimaced, still angry and bitter about the options Raul had laid before her with a cruel air of understanding generosity. If she lived until she was ninety she would not forget her crushing sense of humiliation when Raul had dragged her attraction to him out into the open and squashed her already battered pride.

In Vermont, Raul had evidently seen her susceptibility and quite deliberately steered clear of encouraging her. That awareness now made her feel about a foot high. She had honestly believed that she hadn't betrayed herself, had fondly imagined that she had managed to match his cool and casual manner. She had deliberately avoided every temptation to do otherwise, biting her tongue many, many times in his presence.

She had always left it to him to say when or if he was coming again, had never once complained when he didn't show up, had never attempted to pry into his private life. And, boy, had she been wasting her time in trying to play it cool, she thought now in severe mortification. Raul had been ahead of her. 'Sexual hunger', he had called it! How gallant of him to pretend that he had been tempted too, because she didn't believe that—indeed, not for one second *could* she believe that!

And now she blamed Raul even more bitterly for her own painful misconceptions during that time. Why hadn't he mentioned the existence of other women in his life? Even the most casual reference to another relationship would have put her on her guard. But, no, Raul had been content to allow her to imagine whatever she liked. That had been safer than an honesty that might have made her question his true motive for seeking out her company.

So Raul needn't think that she was going to apologise for telling him that a wedding ring was the only thing likely to persuade her to move to Venezuela. It had been the honest truth. She hadn't expected him to like that truth, or even pause for a second to consider marriage as a possible option to their problem, but she *had* wanted to shock him just as he had shocked her, she conceded uncomfortably.

Yet the raw hostility and dislike she had aroused had not been a welcome result. In fact, his reaction had terrified her, and in retrospect even that annoyed her and filled her with shame. She had to learn to deal with Raul on an impersonal basis.

Raul arrived that evening while she was lying on the sofa watching the film *Pretty Woman*. He strode in at the bit where the heroine was fanning out a selection of condoms for the hero's benefit. Shooting the screen a darkling glance, he said with icy derision, 'I've never understood how a whore could figure as a romantic lead!'

Polly almost fell on the coffee table in her eagerness to grab up the remote control and switch the television off. Hot-cheeked, she looked at him then. He had never seemed more remote: fabulous bone structure taut, lean features cool, his dark and formal business suit somehow increasing his aspect of chilling detachment.

Eyes as black and wintry as a stormy night assailed hers. 'I've applied for a special licence. We'll get married here in forty-eight hours.'

In the act of lifting herself from the sofa, Polly's arms lost their strength and crumpled at the elbows. She toppled back onto the sofa again, a look of complete astonishment fixed to her startled face. 'Say that again—'

'You have made it clear that you will not accept any other option,' Raul drawled flatly.

'But I never expected.... I mean, f-for goodness' sake, Raul,' Polly stammered in severe shock. 'We *can't* just—'

'Can't we? Are you about to change your mind? Are you now prepared to consider allowing me to take my child back home with me?' Raul shot at her.

'No!' she gasped.

'Are you willing to try living in Venezuela on any other terms?'

'No, but—'

'Then don't waste my time with empty protests. You have, after all, just got exactly what you wanted,' Raul informed her icily.

'Not if you feel like this about it,' Polly protested unevenly. 'And it isn't what I precisely wanted—'

'Isn't it? Are you now telling me that you *don't* want me?'

Polly flushed to the roots of her hair, still very sensitive on that subject. 'I... I—'

'If I were you, I wouldn't argue on that point,' Raul warned, a current of threatening steel in his rich, accented drawl. 'In the space of one minute, I could make you eat your words!'

Already in shock, as she was, that level of blunt assurance reduced Polly to writhing discomfiture, but she still said, 'When I mentioned marriage, I didn't mean it as a serious possibility—'

'No, you laid it out as the ultimate price, the ultimate sacrifice.' Raul's hard sensual mouth twisted. 'And I'll get used to the idea. It will be a marriage of convenience, nothing more. I won't allow my child to grow up without me. I also hope I'm not so prejudiced that I can't concede that having both a mother and a father may well be better for the child.'

In a daze of conflicting feelings, Polly muttered, 'But what about... *us*?'

'That baby is the only thing that should matter to either of us. Why should he or she pay the price for this fiasco?'

That was a telling point for Polly. She bowed her head, guilty conscience now in full sway. Only she still couldn't prevent herself from muttering, 'I expected to marry someone who loved me—'

'I didn't expect to marry at all,' Raul traded, without an ounce of sympathy.

'I'll have to think this over—'

'No, you won't. You'll give me your answer now. I'm not in the mood for prima donna tactics!'

Polly experienced a powerful urge to tell him to get lost. And then she thought about being married to Raul, and other, infinitely stronger emotions swamped her. Over time they could work at building up a reasonable relationship, she told herself. They would have the baby to share. Surely their child would help to bring them together? And, all false pride laid aside, Polly was suddenly agonisingly conscious that she would do just about anything to at least have that chance with Raul. If she didn't make that leap of faith now, there would be no second opportunity.

'I'll marry you,' she murmured tautly.

'*Muy bien.*' Raul consulted his watch with disturbing cool. 'I'm afraid I can't stay. I have a dinner engagement.'

'Raul...?'

He turned back from the door.

Polly swallowed hard. 'You can *live* with this option?' she prompted anxiously.

His sudden blazing smile took her completely by surprise, and yet inexplicably left her feeling more chilled than reassured. 'Of course.... I only hope you're equally adaptable.'

Two days later, Polly, clad in a simple white cotton dress, waited in her room for Raul to arrive.

Rod Bevan had told her that he had suggested the courtyard garden for the wedding ceremony, but Raul had apparently wanted a more private setting. Something quick that wouldn't interfere with his busy schedule too much or attract the attention of others, Polly had gathered rather sourly. It was hard to believe that this was her wedding day. No flowers, no guests, nothing that might be construed as an attempt to celebrate the event. Had she been out of her mind to agree to marry Raul?

She had tossed and turned half the night, worrying about that. Absently she rubbed at the nagging ache in the small

of her back. It had begun annoying her around dawn, presumably because she'd been lying in an awkward position.
She felt like a water melon, huge and ungainly. She felt
sorry for herself. She felt tearful. She felt that she might
well be on the brink of making the biggest mistake of her
life.

But Raul himself had put it in a nutshell for her. They
were putting the baby first, and this way their baby would
have two parents. That was very important to Polly, and
she had with constant piety reminded herself of that crucial
fact. There was just one cloud on the horizon…a cloud that
got bigger and blacker every time her conscience stole an
uneasy glance at it.

Raul didn't *want* to marry her. He had made no attempt
to pretend otherwise. The occasional flash of sanity told
Polly that that was all wrong, totally unacceptable as a basis
even for a marriage of convenience. But what was the alternative? Polly couldn't see *any* alternative. Only marriage
could give them both an equal share of their child.

She stretched awkwardly, and used her fingers to mas-
sage the base of her spine. At that moment, Raul strode in.

'*Dios*…let's get this over with as quickly as possible,'
Raul urged impatiently as he reached down a strong hand
to enclose hers and help her up off the sofa.

Thirty seconds later Rod Bevan arrived, accompanied by
two other men. One was the registrar who would perform
the ceremony, the other Raul introduced as his lawyer,
Digby Carson. The service was very brief. When it was
over, everybody shook hands and everybody smiled—with
the exception of Raul. His cool impassivity didn't yield or
melt for a second.

In the midst of an increasingly awkward conversation, a
sharp, tightening sensation formed around Polly's abdo-
men. A stifled gasp was wrenched from her.

'What's wrong?' Raul demanded, anxiety flaring in his
stunning dark eyes.

'I think we'd better forget the coffee and the scones,'

Rod Bevan concluded with a rueful smile as he showed the other two men out.

While he was doing that, Raul scooped Polly up in his arms and laid her down gently on the bed. The impassive look had vanished. His lean, proud face was full of concern. 'The baby's not due for another two weeks,' he told her tautly.

'Babies have their own schedule, Raul. I'd say this one has a pretty good sense of timing,' Rod asserted cheerfully.

'I'll stay with you, Polly,' Raul swore.

'No, you will not!' Polly exclaimed in instantaneous rejection. 'I don't want you with me!'

'I'd like to see my baby born,' Raul murmured intently, staring down at her with all the expectancy his powerful personality could command.

Dumbly she shook her head, tears of embarrassment pricking her eyes. She could not imagine sharing anything that intimate with a man she hadn't even shared a bedroom with.

As he rang the bell for a nurse, she heard the consultant say something in Spanish. Raul's response was quiet, but perceptibly edged by harshness. The door thudded shut on his departure.

'He's furious!' Polly suddenly sobbed, torn by both resentment and an odd, stabbing sense of sharp regret.

'No...he's *hurt*,' the older man contradicted, patting her clenched fingers soothingly. 'For a male as squeamish as Raul, that was one hell of a generous offer!'

Polly gazed down in drowsy fascination at her baby and fell head-over-heels in love for the second time in her life. He was gorgeous. He had fine, silky black hair and big dark eyes, and a cry that seemed to be attached by some invisible string to her heart. He looked so small to her, but the midwife had said he was big—a whole ten pounds one ounce worth of bouncing, healthy baby.

As the nurse settled him into the crib, Raul appeared with

Rod Bevan. Although medication had left Polly feeling
sleepily afloat, and incapable of much in the way of thought
or speech, she stared at Raul in surprise. His darkly handsome features were strained, his expressive mouth taut, his
eyes shadowed. His tie was missing, the jacket of his suit
crumpled and his white shirt open at his strong brown
throat.

'What's wrong?' Polly asked worriedly.

Broodingly, Raul surveyed his sleeping son and thrust a
not quite steady hand through his already rumpled black
hair. 'He's wonderful,' he breathed with ragged appreciation. 'But supremely indifferent to the danger he put you
in!'

The consultant absorbed Polly's frown of incomprehension. 'Raul equates a Caesarean section with a near death
experience,' he explained with gentle satire as he took his
leave in the nurse's wake.

Faint colour overlaid Raul's blunt cheekbones. He studied Polly's weary face and frowned darkly. He reached for
her hand and coiled long fingers warmly round hers. 'I
wasn't prepared for surgical intervention…why didn't you
warn me?'

Polly slowly shook her head.

'Rod tells me you've known for months that the baby
would probably have to be delivered that way,' Raul persisted.

'It's quite common,' Polly managed to slur, her eyelids
feeling as if they had weights driving them downward.

'You're so tiny,' Raul muttered almost fiercely. 'I
should've thought—'

'Bit late now,' Polly incised with drowsy wit.

'My son is beautiful,' Raul murmured. 'At least we got
something right.'

'*Our*…son,' she mumbled.

'We'll call him Rodrigo—'

She winced.

'Jorge?'

She pulled a face.
'Emilio?'
She sighed.
'Luis?'
A faint, drowsy smile curved her lips.
'Luis…Zaforteza,' Raul sounded thoughtfully.
Polly went to sleep.

Polly studied the four confining walls of her room and
smiled. Tomorrow she was leaving the clinic. Her smile
faded, her eyes apprehensive. They were to spend a couple
of days in Raul's apartment and then fly to Venezuela.
Pulling on a luxurious thin silk wrap, she left her room.
Every day Luis went to the nursery for a while to allow
her to rest. Repossessing her son had become the highlight
of her afternoon.

A slight frown line drew her brows together. The day
Luis was born, Raul had seemed so concerned for her, so
approachable, she reflected ruefully. But over the past five
days the barriers had gone up again.

Raul's fascination with his son was undeniable. Yet what
she had believed might bring them closer together seemed
instead to have pushed them further apart. Why was it that
when Raul visited she often felt like a superfluous but extremely well-paid extra? Was it the fact that Raul never
came through the door without some outrageously extravagant gift, which he carelessly bestowed on her in the manner of a rather superior customer bestowing a tip?

Day one, a diamond bracelet. Day two, a half-dozen sets
of luxurious nightwear. Day three, a watch from Cartier.
Day four, a magnificent diamond ring. It had become embarrassing. Raul was rich. Raul was now her husband. But
it felt very strange to be receiving such lavish presents from
a male so cool and distant he never touched her in even
the smallest way.

As she turned the corner into the corridor where the
nursery was, Polly was dismayed to see Raul talking with

Digby Carson outside the viewing window. Neither man having heard her slippered approach, she ducked into an alcove out of sight. She was too self-conscious to join them when she was so lightly clad, and was thoroughly irritated that vanity had made her set aside her more sedate but shabby dressing gown.

'So how do you feel about this…er…development?' the older man was saying quietly, only yards away from her ignominious hiding place.

'Deliriously happy, Digby.'

'Seriously, Raul—'

'That was sarcasm, not humour, Digby. My little bride is much smarter than the average gold-digger,' Raul breathed with stinging bitterness. 'She used my son as a bargaining chip to blackmail me into marriage!'

Rigid with shock at that condemnation, Polly pushed her shoulders back against the cool wall to keep herself upright.

'But whatever happens now I will keep my son,' Raul completed with harsh conviction.

There was a buzzing sound in Polly's ears. She heard the older man say something but she couldn't pick out the words. Dizzily, she shook her head as the voices seemed to recede. When she finally peered out, the corridor was empty again.

Without even thinking about what she was doing, she fled back to the privacy of her room. A gold-digger … a blackmailer. Trembling with stricken disbelief at having heard herself described in such terms, Polly folded down on the bed, no longer sure her wobbly knees would support her.

The pain went deep and then deeper still. Raul despised her. *'Whatever happens now I will keep my son.'* A cold, clammy sensation crawled down Polly's spine. What had he meant by that? And this was the husband she was hoping to make a new life with in Venezuela? A husband who obviously loathed and resented her? In her turmoil, only one fact seemed clear. She could no longer trust Raul…and she couldn't possibly risk taking her son to Venezuela without that trust.

Minutes later, a nurse wheeled in Luis's crib. Seeing Polly already wearing her wrap and slippers, she smiled. 'I see you were just about to come and collect him. Your husband said you were still asleep when he looked in on you earlier, but I know you like to feed Luis yourself.'

Alone with her child again, Polly drew in a shivering, steadying breath. Fear still etched in her shaken eyes, she gazed down at her son's innocent little face, and then she got up in sudden decision.

From the cabinet by the bed she extracted her address book. Leafing frantically through it, she found the phone number her friend Maxie had insisted on giving her when they had parted after the reading of Nancy Leeward's will. 'Liz always knows where I am,' she had promised.

Using the phone by the bed, Polly rang Liz Blake. As soon as the older woman had established who she was, she passed on Maxie's number. When she heard Maxie's familiar husky voice answering her call, Polly felt weak with relief.

'It's Polly...' she muttered urgently. 'Maxie, I need somewhere to stay...'

An hour after that conversation, having left a note of explanation addressed to Raul, Polly walked out of the clinic with Luis in her arms and climbed into the taxi waiting outside. The receptionist was too busy checking in new patients to notice her quiet exit.

# CHAPTER FIVE

POLLY wheeled the stroller in from the roof garden. Threading back her spectacular mane of blonde hair with a manicured hand, Maxie Petronides bent to look in at a warmly-clothed Luis and exclaimed, 'He's so cute I could steal him!'

Polly surveyed her sleeping son with loving eyes. He was four weeks old and he got more precious with every passing day. Remorsefully aware that Raul was being deprived of their son, she had twice sent brief letters containing photos of Luis to Rod Bevan at the clinic, knowing he would pass them on.

The fabulous penthouse flat which she was looking after belonged to Maxie and her husband, Angelos, who used an even more spacious central London apartment. Polly was acting as caretaker for the property while the floors below were transformed into similar luxury dwellings. When the work was complete, Angelos Petronides would put the building on the market with the penthouse as a show home.

'So how are *you* feeling?' Maxie prompted over the coffee that Polly had made.

'Guilty,' Polly confessed ruefully, but she forced a smile, determined not to reveal the real extent of her unhappiness. Every time Raul came into her mind, she forced him out again. He had no business being there. He had *never* had any business being there. Learning to think of Raul only in relation to Luis was a priority.

'You shouldn't be feeling like that,' Maxie reproved. 'You needed this time alone to sort yourself out. This last year, you've been through an awful lot.'

'And made some even more *awful* mistakes,' Polly

71

stressed with a helpless grimace. 'I shouldn't have married Raul. It was incredibly selfish and unfair. I *still* don't know what got into me!'

'Love has a lot to answer for. Sometimes you get so bitter and furious, you want to hit back hard,' Maxie proffered, disconcerting Polly with the depth of her understanding. 'And that just creates more strife. It's only when it all gets too much that you suddenly simmer down and come to your senses.'

'I wish I'd hit that point *before* I married Raul,' Polly muttered wretchedly.

'But Raul has made mistakes too,' Maxie contended firmly. 'He's also sent out some very confusing messages about exactly what he wants from you. But if you're honest with him when you contact him again, it should take some of the heat out of the situation.'

Polly tried to imagine telling Raul that she loved him and just cringed. Some excuse to give a man for forcing him into marrying her! That *was* what she had done, she acknowledged now. And admitting that even to herself still appalled her. But, whether she liked it or not, Raul had had grounds to accuse her of using their son to blackmail him into marriage. That wasn't what she had intended, but that, in his eyes, had been the end result.

In the clinic she had brooded over the hurt and humiliation Raul had carelessly inflicted in Vermont. If she had never seen Raul again she would have got over him eventually, but being forced into such regular contact with him again had plunged her right back into emotional turmoil. She'd been too proud to face up to her continuing feelings for him...a woman scorned? She shuddered at that demeaning label. Whatever, she had been stubbornly blind to what was going on inside her own head.

She had still been so bitterly angry with Raul. Instead of putting those dangerous emotions behind her, before trying to seriously consider their son's future, she had let herself glory in them that day at his apartment. Admittedly, Raul had provoked her with his refusal to even allow that she might be entitled to a life of her own. But marriage would only have been a viable alternative if Raul had been a willing bridegroom.

On their wedding day she had also become a new mother. That in itself would have been quite enough to cope with, but Raul's subsequent behaviour had increased her anxiety about what their future together might hold. That overheard conversation had pushed the misgivings she had been trying to repress and ignore out into the open.

'Initially Angelos wasn't that fussed about getting married either,' Maxie confessed, taking Polly by surprise.

'Did he ever say he would sooner be dead than married?'

'Well, no...'

Of course not. Angelos was besotted with his wife. And Maxie was besotted with her husband. But then Maxie was gorgeous, Polly reflected wryly, and naturally physical attraction had initially brought the couple together. Angelos hadn't looked at Maxie and thought, I *like* her...she'd make a good surrogate mother. So why on earth had she tried to make a comparison?

After Maxie's visit, Polly spent the rest of the day being extremely conscious of the presence of every phone in the apartment. She knew it was time to get in touch with Raul direct. It was now over three weeks since she had left the clinic on a surging tide of rage, pain and fear after hearing Raul's opinion of her. But as that anger had subsided she had gradually come to appreciate that Raul had more right to be bitter than she had initially been prepared to admit.

And at least she now knew what had to be done about the situation, she reflected while she showered in the palatial *en suite* bathroom off the master bedroom. She was ready to humbly acknowledge her mistake, ready to talk to Raul about having their ill-judged marriage annulled. That would put them right back where they had started, but surely it would at least eradicate Raul's hostility? Fearful of the response she was likely to receive, it was after nine that evening when she finally dialled the number Raul had given her weeks earlier in the clinic.

'It's Polly…'

Silence buzzed on the line, and then she heard some background noise she couldn't identify. 'Raul?' she queried uncertainly.

'I heard you,' Raul finally responded, the dark, rich timbre of his accented drawl washing over her with a familiarity that almost hurt. 'Where are you?'

'I thought we should clear the air on the phone first,' Polly admitted tautly. 'Did you get my note?'

'Three pages isn't exactly a "note".'

'I was very upset when I heard you talking about me like that,' Polly admitted tightly.

'I did get that message. But I was letting off steam that day. It never occurred to me that I'd be overheard.'

Polly relaxed slightly.

'Tell me about my son,' Raul urged.

'Could you…could you just once manage to say *our* son?'

'That would be difficult.'

'Why?' Polly pressed.

'"Our" suggests sharing…and right at this minute you are not sharing anything with me,' Raul traded.

Polly paled, but she still coiled round the phone as if it was a fire on an icy night. 'I didn't mean…I didn't *plan* to push you into a marriage you didn't want,' she told him unsteadily.

'You just accidentally fell into that wedding ring, *gatita*?'

Polly turned pink, scrutinising the narrow gold band where it sat in prominent isolation on the coffee table, removed the same day she'd faced up to the fact that it was the symbol of a farce. 'Where are you?'

'In my car…you were saying?' Raul prompted.

'We don't have to stay married!' Polly rushed to make

that point and redeem herself without touching on anything more intimate.

Silence greeted that leading statement.

Polly cleared her throat awkwardly in that interim. 'I suppose you're still very annoyed that I left the clinic…?' Her voice rose involuntarily, turning that sentence into a nervous question.

'It's possible…'

'All of a sudden I didn't feel I could trust you, and I felt trapped…I didn't think I had any alternative—but it was an impulsive decision—'

'You're distressingly prone to impulses, *gatita*,' Raul incised with sudden bite. 'And this dialogue is just irritating the hell out of me!'

The line went dead. With a frown, Polly shook the silent phone. Nothing. Taken aback that Raul should have cut off her call, Polly blinked and slowly straightened. The silence of the apartment enclosed her. Only one soft pool of lamplight illuminated the corner of the big lounge.

Rising, she smoothed down her satin and lace nightgown and went to check on Luis. He was sound asleep, but he was due for a feed soon. In the elegant kitchen she tidied up the remains of her supper and prepared a bottle for Luis. All the time she was doing that, she agonised over that conversation with Raul. He had sounded so strange. Strained, wary, then bitingly angry.

The doorbell went, making her jump and then as quickly relax again. Maxie was her only visitor, and Maxie had called in one other evening, when Angelos had had a business dinner. Polly hurried across the octagonal hall. Without bothering to use the intercom, she hit the release button on the security lock which barred access to the private lift in the underground car park.

Then she stilled with a frown. Why would Maxie come to see her twice in one day? Only if there was something wrong! Running an apprehensive hand through the fall of her mahogany hair, Polly waited impatiently. It seemed ages before she heard the low, distant hum of the approaching lift, then the soft ping as it reached the top floor. The doors purred back.

But it was *not* Maxie; it was Raul who strode out of the lift.

Polly went into startled retreat, aghast eyes pinned to his intimidatingly tall and powerfully male physique.

Scathing dark-as-night eyes flashed into hers. '*Dios mio*…you deserve a bloody good fright!' Raul informed her wrathfully. 'All that high tec security and you don't even *check* who your visitor is before you invite him up?'

In shock, Polly felt her teeth chatter together. 'I…I just assumed it was Maxie—'

'Don't you have any sense? I could've been a rapist, or a robber, and I bet you're alone in this apartment!'

Swallowing hard, Polly gave a jerky nod, her attention fully locked to him. He looked spectacular in a fabulous silver-grey suit, cut to enhance every sleek, muscular angle of his wide-shouldered, lean-hipped and long-legged frame. As her shaken gaze ran over him, her stomach flipped and her mouth ran dry. His magnetic dark good looks were like a visual assault on senses starved of him.

'How…how did you find out where I was?' Her bewilderment was unconcealed.

Raul's wide mouth curled with impatience. 'Once I had your phone number, it was a piece of cake to get the address. Why do you think I kept you on the line for so long?'

Since Polly hadn't been conscious until the end of that call that anyone but her had been controlling anything, she gulped.

'Angelos Petronides will answer to me for this,' Raul breathed with sudden chilling conviction, lean, strong face forbidding.

'Angelos… Maxie's husband? You *know* him?' Polly exclaimed in surprise.

'Of course I know him, and he owns this building. Here you are on Petronides ground. I thought better of Angelos.

I didn't think he'd get involved in hiding my wife from me, but now that he *has*—'

'No, he hasn't!' Polly protested vehemently. 'I've never even met Maxie's husband! I asked her to help me find somewhere to stay and she brought me here—said they needed someone to look after the place. Maxie's certainly not aware that you know Angelos. And, as I asked her to be discreet, she's only told Angelos that she has an old friend staying here for a while…'

As her voice faltered to a halt, she experienced the feeling that she had already lost Raul's full attention. As his dark golden gaze roamed over her scantily clad figure, Polly suddenly became intensely conscious of the revealing nature of her nightgown, the delicate straps which exposed her bare shoulders, the sheer lace covering her breasts, the light, clinging fabric which outlined her once-again-slim hips and slender thighs for his appraisal.

As the silence which had seemed to come out of nowhere pulsed, Polly felt her breasts swell with languorous heaviness. Her nipples pinched tight, as if a current of fire had touched them. As she folded her arms over herself in mortified discomfiture, she snapped, 'Has anybody ever told you that it's very rude to stare?'

The silence lay still and impenetrable as glass.

And then Raul flung his darkly handsome head back and laughed with a rich spontaneity that shook Polly. Laughter put to flight his gravity, throwing his innate charisma to the fore. Her heart lurched. She tried to give him a reproving look, needing him to show her a mood she recognised and stay in it long enough for her to respond accordingly. But at that moment she was like a novice actress without a script and unable to improvise.

'You've gone from voluptuously ripe and enticing to sinfully, sexily slender,' Raul murmured with husky amusement. 'And you think it's *rude* that I should stare at my own wife?'

A deep flush lit Polly's fair skin. She didn't know where

to look, but was pretty sure she was not going to look back at him while he was saying things like that. *Sinfully, sexily slender?* Now she knew what Maxie had meant when she had criticised Raul for giving her conflicting messages. An impersonal and detached relationship had to have firm boundaries. Raul had been both impersonal and detached after their wedding, politely concerned that she should be comfortable and content, but nothing more. He had made no attempt to behave like a normal husband who had a relationship with the mother of his child.

And then Polly called herself an idiot. Here she was, wondering why Raul was behaving so strangely! But wouldn't most men react differently to a woman standing around half-naked in front of them? Hot colour flooded her cheeks at that obvious explanation.

'I'll go and put something on and then we can talk,' Polly muttered in a rush.

'Let me see Luis first,' Raul countered, moving closer to catch her hand and check her before she could move.

'You're not still annoyed with Maxie's husband, are you?' Polly asked anxiously as she took him down the corridor.

'I have a certain tolerance for a man plunged unsuspecting into an embarrassing situation by his bride,' Raul imparted wryly. 'Angelos is Greek, traditional as they come. He'd come down on his wife like a ton of bricks if he realised that she'd been helping to hide *my* wife and child from me!'

'It wasn't like that—'

'Only violence or abuse on my part would justify such interference between a man and his wife.'

Was that the third or the fourth time that Raul had referred to her as *his wife* in as many minutes? Polly thought abstractedly. After three weeks of telling herself that their marriage was a pathetic charade, it seemed so odd to have Raul referring to her in such terms.

'Raul...I really needed some time and space to think,' she murmured tautly.

Raul released her hand. 'You've had months to think without me around.'

But their relationship had changed radically in recent weeks, Polly wanted to protest in frustration as she watched him fluidly cross the elegant guest room to where Luis lay in his cradle. Their marriage had been one of reckless haste, entered into without proper consideration or adequate discussion.

She hadn't simply taken umbrage and run away; she had known that ultimately she would have to face Raul again and deal with the situation.

But in her distress and turmoil she had been in no fit state to confront a male who had a naturally domineering and powerful personality—and, worst of all, a male who had everything to gain from putting pressure on her to still accompany him to Venezuela. She had known she had to have time to think away from Raul before she decided what to do next.

Raul sent her a cool, assessing glance. 'I've known Digby all my life. What you heard was a private conversation with a friend. I imagine you and your friend Maxie have been less than charitable about me on at least *one* recent occasion...'

Unprepared for that embarrassingly accurate stab, Polly was betrayed by the burning wave of colour which swept up her throat.

'*Exactly,*' Raul purred with rich satisfaction, removing his attention from her to study his infant son, who was squirming into wakefulness. 'Do you see me getting all worked up about a fact of life? Could you see me writing three vitriolic pages and vanishing into thin air on such slender proof of intent as the mood of a moment?'

'No, but—'

'There is no "but",' Raul broke in with derision. 'Only

women behave like that. Rod thought it might be the baby blues, or some such thing! I knew better.'

'I was in the wrong…I should've confronted you,' Polly conceded tightly, heart-shaped face fixed in a mutinous expression, revealing the struggle it was to voice those words of contrition.

'Instead of throwing a tantrum on paper,' Raul emphasised, subjecting her to a hard, steady appraisal. 'Because I warn you now, I will never, ever allow you to be in a position again where you can use our son as a weapon against me.'

At that opportune moment, Luis mustered his lungs into a cross little cry for attention. Pale and taut now, in receipt of that menacing warning, Polly was grateful for the opportunity to turn away. But Raul reached his son first, sweeping him up with complete confidence. Smiling down at Luis, he talked to him in soft, soothing Spanish.

In the blink of an eye Raul had gone from that chilling threat to an unashamed display of tenderness with their son, Polly registered. That was the most intimidating thing to watch—the speed and ease with which he could switch emotional channels. Although there had been nothing emotional about his determination to tell her how he felt about her flight from the clinic. Cool, scornful, cutting.

'I'll get his bottle,' Polly muttered.

She skidded down to the bedroom to pull on a fluttering silk wrap first. When she returned to the dimly lit bedroom, Raul rose from the armchair to let her take a seat. He settled Luis into her arms and then hunkered lithely down to watch his son greedily satisfy his hunger.

'*Dios mío!* No wonder he's grown so much!'

Polly cleared her throat awkwardly. 'I want you to know that I would never use Luis as a weapon—'

'You already have,' Raul told her without hesitation, smoothing an astonishingly gentle hand over Luis's little head before vaulting upright again. 'In disputes between couples, the child is often a weapon. You should understand that as well as I do. When your parents' marriage broke up, your father kept you and your mother apart. Why? He was punishing her for leaving him for another man.'

Polly was astonished that he should still recall that much information about her background. 'I suppose he was,' she conceded as she got up to change Luis.

'Love turns to hatred so easily. It never lasts,' Raul murmured with supreme cynicism.

'It lasts for a lot of people,' Polly argued abstractedly, down on her knees and busily engaged in dealing with her son's needs. But she gathered courage from not being forced to meet Raul's often unsettling gaze. 'You know what I said on the phone earlier...about us not having to stay married?'

Having expected an immediate response to that reminder, Polly looked up in the resounding silence which followed.

Raul was staring back at her with penetrating and grim eyes. 'I do.'

'Look, why don't you wait in the lounge while I settle Luis?' Polly suggested uncomfortably.

A few minutes later, Luis was back in the cradle, snug and comfy and sleepy.

'I love you, you precious baby,' Polly whispered feelingly, not looking forward to the discussion she was about to open but convinced that Raul would be extremely relieved when she suggested that they have their marriage annulled.

As she entered the lounge, Raul swung round from the fireplace. 'I don't like this room. It's claustrophobic with that conservatory built over the windows,' he said with flat distaste. 'It's insane to close out such magnificent views!'

'Maxie's terrified of heights. That's why it's like that...' Polly hovered awkwardly. 'Raul—?'

'I'm not giving you a divorce,' Raul delivered before she could say another word.

Was he thinking angrily about the prospect of having to offer a divorce settlement? Did he imagine she was planning to make some greedy, gold-digging claim on his legendary wealth?

Polly reddened with annoyance at that suspicion. 'We don't need to go for a divorce. We can apply for an annulment and everything will be put right. It will be like this wretched marriage of ours never happened.'

Raul had gone very still, dark eyes narrowing into watchful and wary arrows of light in his dark, devastating face. 'An annulment?' he breathed, very low, that possibility evidently not having occurred to him.

'Well, why not?' Polly asked him tautly. 'It's the easiest way out.'

'Let me get this straight...' Raul spread two lean brown hands with silent fluency to express apparent astonishment. 'Just one short month ago you married me, and now, without living a *single* day with me, you have changed your mind?'

'You're making me sound really weird,' Polly muttered in reproach. 'I was wrong to let you marry me, knowing that you didn't want that option. Now I'm admitting it—'

'But too late...you're admitting it too late,' Raul declared.

'But it's not too late...' Polly's brow furrowed with confusion, because the discussion was not going in the direction she had expected. 'It's not as if we've lived together...or anything like that. Why are you looking at me like I'm crazy? You don't *want* to be married to me.'

As he listened to that stumbling reminder, dark colour flared over Raul's slashing cheekbones and his stunning dark eyes suddenly blazed gold. 'But I have come to terms with the fact that I *am* married to you!'

'I think we both deserve a bit more than that out of marriage,' Polly opined in growing discomfiture. 'We rushed into it—'

'*I* didn't rush,' Raul interrupted. 'I just wanted to get it over with!'

'Yes, well...doesn't it strike you that that isn't a promising basis for *any* marriage?' Polly framed carefully, alarmingly awake to the angry tension emanating from his tall, commanding figure. 'I thought you'd be pleased at the idea of having your freedom back.'

'Freedom is a state of mind. I now see no reason why marriage should make the slightest difference to my life,' Raul returned with grating assurance.

Polly was momentarily silenced by that sweeping statement.

'You're my wife, and the mother of my son. I suggest you get used to those facts of life,' Raul completed, studying her in angry, intimidating challenge.

A bemused look now sat on Polly's face. Her lashes fluttered. The tip of her tongue crept out to nervously moisten the taut fullness of her lower lip. 'I don't understand...'

Hooded eyes of gleaming gold dropped to linger on the ripe pink contours of her mouth. 'Sometimes you talk too much, *gatita*...'

'What does that mean...that word you keep on using?' Polly whispered, because the very atmosphere seemed to sizzle, warning her of the rise in tension. Suddenly she was finding it very difficult to breathe.

'*Gatita?*' Raul laughed as he closed the distance between them in one easy stride. 'It means "kitten". The shape of your face, those big blue eyes...you remind me of a little fluffy cat, cute and soft with unexpected claws.'

Having spent a lifetime fighting the downside of being smaller than most other people, Polly was not best pleased to be linked with any image described by words like 'little', 'fluffy' or 'cute'.

'What do you think I am? Some kind of novelty?' she demanded, fighting not to be intimidated by his proximity and towering height.

'If I knew what it was that attracts me to you, the attraction probably would have died by now,' Raul said cynically.

Polly stilled, feathery brows drawing together. 'But you're *not* attracted to me...'

Raul dealt her a rampantly amused appraisal. 'I may have controlled my baser urges, but I've lost count of the times I almost succumbed to the temptation of hauling you into my arms in Vermont,' he admitted frankly. 'Then I believed your appeal was related to the simple fact that I knew you were carrying *my* child...'

'Yes?' Polly conceded breathlessly, with the aspect of a woman struggling to take a serious academic interest in a confession that had flung her brain into wild confusion. Her heart was now thumping like a manic hammer below her breastbone.

'But now I've finally worked out what got us into this in the first place,' Raul confided, and, without giving her a hint of his intentions, he lifted his hands and slowly tipped the wrap from her taut shoulders. 'Subconsciously I picked you to be Luis's mother because you appealed to my hormones... Once I'd reached that conclusion, suddenly everything that's gone wrong between us started making sense!'

In her complete bemusement at that declaration, Polly was standing so still the garment simply slid down her arms and pooled on the carpet. 'What...*what*?' she began with a nervous start.

Bending, Raul closed his strong arms round her and almost casually swept her up off her feet.

*'What are you doing?'* Polly shrieked in sheer shock.

Raul dealt her a slashing smile of unashamed satisfaction. 'Husbands don't need to control their baser urges.'

'Put me down—'

But Raul silenced that angry command by bringing his hungry mouth crashing down on hers without further ado.

Polly saw stars. Stars inside her head, stars exploding like hot sunbursts in all sorts of embarrassing places inside her. It wasn't like the only other kiss they had shared—a slow burner, cut off before it reached its height. Raul's devouring demand had an instant urgency this time, intensifying her own shaken response. He probed her mouth with tiny little darting stabs of his tongue. The raw sexuality of that intimate assault was shockingly effective. It set up a chain reaction right through her whole body, filling her with a wild, wanton need for more.

Polly uttered a strangled moan low in her throat, hands sweeping up to dig possessively into his luxuriant black hair and hold him to her. Without warning, Raul broke free to raise his head, dark golden eyes intent on her hectically flushed face as he strode out into the hall and started down the corridor. '*Dios*…I could make love to you all night, but I know you're not ready for that yet,' he groaned in frank frustration.

Surfacing in turmoil from that predatory kiss, Polly gasped, 'Where on earth do you think you're taking me?'

Unerringly finding the master bedroom, opposite the guest room in which Luis slept, Raul shouldered wide the door, strode across the carpet and deposited her with almost exaggerated gentleness on the vast divan bed. He hit the light switch by the bed, dimly illuminating the room. Then he straightened with an indolent smile.

Polly reared up, bracing herself on her hands, her hair tumbling round her pink cheeks, her eyes very blue as she studied him in shaken disbelief. 'Do you honestly think I'm about to go to bed with you?'

It didn't take Raul two seconds to respond to that question. Surveying her steadily, he jerked loose his silk tie. '*Sí*…you're my wife.'

'This is not a normal marriage!' Polly argued, still gazing at him with very wide and incredulous eyes.

'That's been our biggest problem. The sooner this marriage becomes "normal" the better,' Raul delivered, discarding his tie and sliding fluidly out of his jacket to pitch it on a nearby chair. 'It's time to forget how we started out—'

'But we didn't start *anything*!' Polly slung back, watch-

ing him unbutton his tailored silk shirt with the transfixed
aspect of a woman unable to credit that he was actually
undressing in front of her. 'I was pregnant before we even
met!'

'Stop complicating things. You were pregnant with my
baby. That created a special intimacy from the outset.
Naturally that made a difference to how I reacted to you—'

'In Vermont?' Polly threw in helplessly. 'When you
dropped in out of the blue whenever it suited you?'

'It's difficult to be casual any other way.'

'I bet you *always* suit yourself!' Polly condemned thinly.

Raul gave her a wondering and decidedly amused appraisal. 'Five-foot-nothing tall and you're nagging at me
like a little shrew!' he marvelled.

Polly could feel her temper rising like a rocket desperate
to go into orbit. 'I want you to treat me seriously, Raul.'

'Then say something relevant to the present,' he advised
rather drily. 'Vermont was months ago. Vermont was when
I still believed I was going to collect my child and walk
away. We've moved on a lot since then.'

He peeled off his shirt.

Polly stared, throat closing, tongue cleaving to the roof
of her dry mouth. He was incredibly beautifully built. All
sleek bronzed skin and muscles, a hazy triangle of dark
curls sprinkling his impressive torso. She blushed and
averted her eyes. 'I'm not ready to share a bedroom with
you yet,' she informed him tautly.

'I'm ready enough for both of us,' Raul said with amused
assurance.

Without looking at him, Polly sat forward and linked her
hands round her upraised knees. 'But I wasn't prepared for
this... Before you came here tonight, I thought we'd be
applying for an annulment to *end* our marriage,' she reminded him tensely. 'And sex isn't something I can treat
casually—'

'*Bueno*...I'm delighted to hear it.'

'And...I haven't done this before,' Polly completed jerkily.

The silence spread for endless seconds that clawed cruelly at her nerves.

'*Como?*' Raul breathed in a near whisper.

Polly snatched in a shaky breath and simply squeezed her eyes tight shut. 'I've never had a lover.'

'That's not possible,' Raul informed her.

'Yes it is!' Polly said, almost fiercely in her embarrassment, desperate to drop the subject but registering by his audibly shattered responses that there was no current prospect of an easy escape.

'Look at me!' Raul commanded.

Her hot face a study of mingled chagrin and resentment, Polly glanced up and collided with incredulous dark golden eyes. 'Some women *don't* sleep around!' she snapped.

Raul moved closer to the bed, his frowning bemusement doing nothing to reduce her suspicion that he now saw her as some kind of freak. 'But you were at university...you must've had at least *one* relationship.'

'Not a physical one. I don't believe in intimacy without commitment,' Polly admitted stiffly, doggedly fighting her own discomfiture. 'And "commitment" is a dirty word to a lot of men these days. I may be out of step with the times, but I'm not ashamed of my views.'

'Technically still a virgin,' Raul murmured sibilantly, letting his glittering golden gaze roam over her with hungry intent. 'I'm very surprised—but, since I shall be your first lover, I think I can handle the situation. And, as my wife, you can hardly question the level of *my* commitment.'

That proud and confident assurance hovered there for a split second. Polly lost colour and dragged her troubled eyes from him to focus on the bare pink toes which protruded from below the hem of her nightgown. 'But you didn't *want* that commitment,' she reminded him in a strained tone.

'I'll get used to it.'

Polly swallowed hard and took her courage in both hands, determined to go to the heart of her misgivings and be frank. 'But if we share a bed, Raul...I expect you to be faithful.'

The silence thickened and lay heavily.

'No woman tells me what to do,' Raul countered with ferocious bite. 'And that includes you!'

Polly froze, and then stared at the fancy silk bedspread until it blurred below her shaken eyes. Then she angled her head back and forced herself to meet the onslaught of his chilling dark eyes. 'I think fidelity is the least commitment you could make.'

'*Dios...*' Raul growled, reaching for his discarded shirt in an abrupt movement and pulling it back on. 'So you have found another weapon. Off the top of my head I could name a dozen married men and women cheating on their spouses...do you think *they* didn't make promises?'

Polly's heart was beating so fast it felt as if it was sitting at the foot of her throat. 'But that's not—'

'This marriage is on trial, as every new relationship is. Do you think living together like brother and sister is a fair test of any relationship between a man and a woman?' Raul derided with lancing scorn, black eyes raking mercilessly over her disconcerted face. 'Do you fondly imagine that I will be a good little celibate boy while you sit back and smugly weigh up whether or not you can trust me enough to reward me with the right to share your bed?'

'I didn't mean it like that, Raul!' Polly argued strickenly as she sprang off the bed.

'So far you have had everything your way, but here it stops,' Raul delivered, his cold rage unconcealed. 'If you refuse to behave like a normal wife, *don't* expect me to behave like a husband!'

Shocked and distressed by the savage anger she had provoked, Polly clutched at his arm as he reached for his jacket, 'Raul, I—'

He swung back and closed a powerful arm round her

slight body, imprisoning her. He meshed long fingers into her hair, forcing her eyes to meet his. 'First you bargain with my son, then you bargain with sex.'

Breathless and trembling, she gazed up at him, lost herself in the brilliance of his shimmering dark eyes. *'No!'* she protested painfully.

Bending, Raul slid his arm below her slim hips and lifted her unceremoniously up to his level, crushing her swelling breasts into the muscular wall of his chest. Her nostrils flared on the enervating, hot, husky male scent of him. Hard black eyes assailed hers and held them by pure force of personality. 'You will not dictate terms to me. You will not demand empty and meaningless guarantees. A proper wife doesn't put a price on her body!'

'I...I wasn't doing that—'

'The marriage is on trial...*I am not!*' Raul stressed forcefully. 'I will not be judged on the basis of my past!'

Polly couldn't get breath into her lungs. Soft lips parting, she snatched in tiny little pants, drowning against her volition in the power of those compelling dark eyes.

'You're such a little hypocrite,' Raul delivered in a contemptuous undertone, scanning her dilated pupils and flushed cheeks. A sensually intent glitter flared in his assessing gaze, giving him the look of a tiger about to spring as he cupped her chin, lean fingers lingering to smoothly stroke the smooth curve of her jaw. 'This close to me, you're like a stick of dynamite hoping for a match!'

'I don't know what you're talking about—'

Striding over to the bed, Raul lowered her and followed her down onto the divan in one smooth, lithe motion. 'Then let me *show* you...'

Before she could even guess his intention, he had anchored her in place with one long, powerful thigh and brought his hard, mobile mouth crashing down on hers. With his tongue he plundered the sensitive interior with raw, erotic thoroughness. She groaned, plunged helplessly into the grip of mindless pleasure. He slid a hand beneath her, arching her up into contact with the aggressive thrust of his arousal, sending a cascade of fire trickling through her veins to accelerate every pulse.

Raul lifted his head. Her eyes were dazed, her ripe mouth reddened and swollen. Looking up at that lean, strong face, she trembled, caught up in a spell she was too weak to fight. With a slumberous smile, Raul flicked loose the tiny pearl buttons on the lace bodice of her nightie. And all the time Polly was involuntarily watching *him*, studying the black density and length of the lashes fanning his high cheekbones—the sole feminising influence in those hard-boned features—the luxuriant ebony hair tumbled by her fingers on to his brow, the blue-black shadow already roughening his strong jawline. All male, stunningly sexy.

'You have beautiful breasts,' Raul sighed.

Disconcerted, she followed the direction of his gaze. Thunderstruck, she stiffened and flushed at the sight of her own breasts, rising bare and shameless for his appraisal, her nipples already distended into wanton pink buds. 'Raul...?' she mumbled unevenly, lying there, wanting to cover herself, wanting to move, and yet inexplicably powerless to attempt to do either.

He allowed his thumb to delicately rub over one prominent peak, and her whole body jerked on the wave of sudden sensation that made her teeth grit in sensual shock and fired an insistent throb between her thighs.

'And you are *so* responsive,' he husked, angling back from her and then, without any warning whatsoever, smoothly sliding off the bed to spring upright again.

She suddenly found herself lying there alone and exposed, and a muffled cry of dismay escaped Polly. She rolled over onto her stomach, shaken, bewildered eyes pinned to Raul. Hooking his jacket on one forefinger, he glanced back at her from the door, bronzed face saturnine, black eyes several degrees below freezing.

'I could take you any time I wanted...and I *will*,' he swore, soft and low.

'You can't make me do anything I don't want to do!'

'Oh, yes, I can, *gatita*. Haven't the last five minutes taught you anything?' Raul skimmed back with merciless cool. 'You have an amazing capacity to lose yourself in passion. By the time I'm finished with you, you will be begging me to share the marital bed!'

Polly was already so devastated by what he had just done to her that she just gaped at him, heart sinking like a stone, stomach clenching sickly. A cruelly humiliating and deliberate demonstration of sexual power from a male who had homed in like a predator on her one weakness. *Him.* She was appalled by a depth of diabolic calculation alien to her own more open nature.

'A car will pick you up tomorrow evening. We're flying home,' Raul drawled indolently as he sauntered out through the door. '*Buenas noches*, Señora Zaforteza.'

She listened to him walk down the corridor, her hands bunched into fists. She wanted to scream with angry frustration and pain. She hated him, but she hated herself more. He had kissed her and nothing else had mattered. Now her body ached with guilty, unfulfilled passion, the enemy of every fine principle she had ever believed in. She was finally finding out how hard it was to withstand physical temptation.

And Raul? she thought furiously. Raul had simply walked away, content to have made his point in the most ego-crushing manner available.

## CHAPTER SIX

POLLY sat in a comfortable seat in the spacious cabin of Raul's private jet and suppressed a sigh. Luis was asleep in his skycot and Raul had still to arrive. He had been delayed.

She glanced curiously at Irena, the young and pretty stewardess watching out for Raul's arrival. A sultry brunette, she looked like a model in her smart uniform, but in spite of the long wait she had coolly avoided any real contact with her employer's wife. A man's woman, uninterested in her own sex, Polly had decided.

Hearing the sound of feet on the metal steps outside, seeing Irena's face blossom into surprising warmth as she moved out of view to greet Raul, Polly was annoyed to recognise her own powerful sense of anticipation—and, mortifyingly, her childish stab of envy that the brunette should get to see him first. Swallowing hard on that lowering awareness, she studied the carpet, fighting to contain her own dangerously volatile emotions.

'Sorry, I'm late...' Raul drawled with infuriating cool, crossing the cabin to peruse his slumbering son and comment, in a tone of satisfaction and pride, 'Luis is always so peaceful.'

'You've never seen him any other way. Actually, your son kept me up half the night!' Polly complained thinly, before she could think better of it.

Disorientatingly, Raul laughed as he sank lithely down opposite her, forcing her to look at him for the first time. And his sheer stunning impact simply slaughtered her carefully prepared outer shield of tranquillity. Last night he had finally ripped away her defences and made her betray herself in his arms. Now she discovered there could be no pretense of indifference or detachment, not when her nails were already digging painfully into her palms, her skin dampening, her breathing quickening, her eyes unable to rest any place but on him.

Those bronzed features, already as familiar to her as her own yet still possessed of the most intense charismatic appeal. The lean, arrogant nose, the spectacular dark, deep-set eyes, the wide, hard mouth, the aggressive jawline. Drop-dead gorgeous, and yet every angle of that darkly handsome face was stamped with immense strength and character.

'At the *hato*...the ranch, the whole household will revolve round our son,' Raul promised with quiet amusement. 'He will be spoiled by so many willing helpers that your nights should be undisturbed from now on.'

Polly could see no reflection of her own highwire tension in him. He talked briefly, lightly about their destination. The isolated ranch where his ancestors had lived for generations was on the cattle plains he called the *llanos*. It would be very hot, possibly quite wet as the rainy season wasn't quite over yet, Raul warned in the sort of bracing, healthy, dismissive tone she suspected the hardy might use to refer to a hellhole they loved and honoured as home, regardless of its deficiencies.

Soon after the jet had taken off, Raul released his belt and leant forward to unsnap Polly's. Rising, he curved strong hands over her taut shoulders to urge her up into the circle of his arms.

'What are you—?'

'Lesson one on being a proper wife,' Raul murmured with amused dark eyes as he scanned her bewildered face. 'Even when you're really mad at me, you should always look glad to see me when we've been apart.'

That close to that lithe, lean body, Polly trembled. 'You are so changeable,' she condemned shakily. 'You were furious with me last night—'

'I'm just not used to a negative response in the bedroom,' Raul countered with velvet-soft satire. 'And when I've been forced to ride roughshod over my every reservation to become a legally wedded husband, that negative response took some swallowing.'

'But I tried to explain how I felt—'

'Not with an explanation I can take seriously, Polly,' Raul interrupted with conviction. 'You want me. I want you. You have a wedding ring to satisfy your principles. Sex is only a physical hunger, an appetite...not something important enough to become a divisive issue between us.'

Polly blinked, striving to think that through and shrinking from the feelings she experienced in response. *Not important?* An appetite, something to be casually, even carelessly satisfied as and when the need took him? Such terminology ensured that there was little danger of her overestimating the extent of her own attractions, she conceded in fierce pain.

A firm hand caught her chin, tipping up her face, making her meet the passionate gold of his intent gaze. 'If you expect too much from me, I am certain to disappoint you. Don't do that to us. Be satisfied with what we have,' Raul warned almost roughly.

Polly flung her head back. 'And what *do* we have?'

In answer, he attacked on her weakest flank. He lifted her up into his powerful arms, his sensual mouth took hers and she was lost, filled with the mindless pleasure of simply being there. All she was capable of at that moment was feeling—feeling what *he* could make her feel. The wild, sweet excitement as seductive as a drug, the shivering sensitivity of her own body crushed into the wonderfully masculine strength of his, heady sensation born at every point where they touched.

He released her lips and she discovered she was sprawled across his lap like a wanton, without any memory of how she had got there. Struggling to catch her breath, she stared into the stunning eyes level with her own. Long brown fingers framed her flushed cheekbones and eased her back from him.

'At least we have a starting point, *gatita*. It will be enough,' Raul swore with silken satisfaction. 'Now I think you should get some rest.'

'Rest?' she repeated unevenly.

'You look exhausted, and this is a very long flight.'

'Luis...?' she mumbled.

'I can manage him for a few hours,' Raul asserted with cool confidence.

Polly scrambled clumsily upright again, face burning under the onslaught of a wave of hot colour. Her legs were so wobbly she wasn't sure she could walk, and she felt dizzy, disorientated.

Raul watched her retreat to the sleeping compartment every step of the way, a slightly amused smile beginning to curve his expressive mouth. Polly shut the door and sagged, furious with him, furious with herself. First he treated her like a toy to be played with, then he dismissed her like a child after a goodnight kiss! It made her feel controlled and horribly vulnerable, because she literally didn't know at any given time what Raul was planning to do next. Just because he was experienced...and she wasn't!

Oh, dear heaven, no, she reflected, not wanting to even think about how and where he had gained all that cool sexual assurance. She curled up in a tight ball on the built-in bed. Until Raul had said it, she hadn't realised just how very tired she was. Hopefully she would be better equipped to deal with him when she felt a little more buoyant.

Polly woke up slowly, eyes opening blankly on her surroundings until she finally registered that she was still on the Zaforteza jet. Glancing at her watch, she groaned in disbelief. She had just enjoyed the equivalent of a full night's sleep for the first time since Luis had been born...*Luis!* Pushing her wildly tumbled hair off her brow,

Polly rolled off the bed and opened the door back into the main cabin.

A cosy and unexpected little scene met her startled eyes. Chattering in soft, intimate Spanish, Irena was leaning over Raul while he cradled Luis. She was as close to Raul as a lover. Her big brown eyes swept Polly's sleep-flushed face and crumpled clothing in a hostile look at the interruption.

'Why didn't you wake me up sooner?' Polly demanded curtly of Raul.

'You were exhausted, and Irena was happy to help out.' As Raul ran his stunning dark eyes over her tousled appearance, his ebony brows drew together in a slight but highly effective frown. 'You should get changed. We'll be landing at Maiquetia in an hour.'

The stewardess still had one possessive hand resting on Raul's shoulder. Polly was appalled to register that the source of her own ferocious tension was undeniably a hot nasty jealousy which fuelled instantly suspicious thoughts. What had they been doing all those hours while she was asleep and safely out of the way? Was that why Raul had been so keen to send her off to rest? Why did Irena look like a cat that had got the cream?

As Polly studied Raul with a highly combustible mix of suspicion, distrust and embittered shameful longing, he stood up and calmly settled their son into his neat little cot. 'I need a shave.'

'Did you get *any* sleep?' Polly muttered tautly.

'Enough. I don't need much.' Raul strode past her.

'Your husband is a real dynamo, *señora*. He has worked for most of the flight,' the young stewardess shared with a coy look of admiration, tossing her head with a husky little laugh. 'But don't worry, I ensured that he ate and took time out to relax.'

At that news, Polly paled and went back into the sleeping compartment, but Raul had already disappeared into the compact bathroom next door. She lifted the white lightweight dress she had laid out earlier and smoothed abstractedly at the remaining creases while she waited for Raul to emerge. Finally the door opened. She felt absolutely sick by then, suspicion and jealousy making mincemeat of all rational thought.

'Do you sleep with Irena?' That blunt question just erupted from Polly. It was inside her head, but she could not for the life of her work out how the question had got from her brain onto her tongue.

Raul studied her without any expression at all. 'Tell me you didn't ask me that.'

That eerie lack of reaction completely spooked Polly. She crimsoned, pinned her lips together and then opened them again, driven by an overwhelming need for reassurance. 'After what you said the night before last about not behaving like a husband...not to mention the way *she's* behaving around you...naturally I'm suspicious!'

'If I answer that insanely stupid question, I will lose my temper with you,' Raul warned, very soft and low, narrowed dark eyes flaming gold between lush black lashes.

'I don't trust you—'

'I will not live with jealous scenes. In fact nothing would disgust me more or alienate me faster. I do not sleep with my employees. The only woman in my life at present is you,' Raul stated with a feral flash of even white teeth which suggested that even making that admission went severely against the grain.

Polly relaxed ever so slightly. 'I want to believe that, but—'

'The truth is that *you* are jealous of Irena,' Raul condemned with whiplash cool. 'Could that be because she makes the effort to look like an attractive adult woman while you're still dressing like an adolescent who doesn't want to grow up?'

Utterly unprepared for that counter-attack, Polly felt her soft mouth fall wide.

Raul flicked the white sundress off the bed. 'A three-year-old could wear this! Embroidered flowers at the neck-line, ruched, shapeless—'

'It *was* bought in a children's department. Ordinary shops don't cater for women my height and size!' Polly shot at him shakily. 'And, since I don't want to dress like a precocious teenybopper, I have to choose the plain out-fits.'

Raul shrugged. 'OK...I'll remedy that.'

'I am not jealous of *that woman*...and you needn't think you can change the subject—'

'Oh, I'm not changing it, Polly...I'm just refusing to talk about it,' Raul incised with sudden grimness, shooting her a coldly derisive look. 'Use your brain. Irena is Venezuelan. Venezuelan women are naturally glamorous, confident and flirtatious—'

'My goodness, I can hardly wait to meet the Venezuelan men! What a fun time I'm going to have in your country!' Polly forecast furiously.

In a sudden movement that shook Polly inside out, Raul strode forward and closed a lean and powerful hand round her slender forearm, dwarfing her with his intimidating height and breadth. With his other hand, he pushed up her chin, subjecting her to a splintering look of burning outrage that made her stomach turn an abrupt somersault and her knees go weak and wobbly.

'What is mine is *mine*,' Raul stressed with barely sup-pressed savagery. 'I'd break you into little pieces for the jaguar to feed on before I would let any other man near you!'

Plunged willy-nilly into an atmosphere suddenly raw with scorching lightning currents of threat, Polly simply gazed up at him like a stupefied rabbit.

With equal abruptness, Raul released her again, a be-traying rise of blood delineating his proud cheekbones as he absorbed her bewilderment. 'I'm not a jealous man,' he asserted in a roughened undertone. 'But I am very conscious of my honour, and of my son's need for stability in his life.'

Polly nodded like a little wooden marionette, afraid to move too close to the hungry flickering flames of a bonfire.

Raul was pale now beneath his golden skin, his superb bone structure harshly prominent. 'I'm sorry if I overreacted...'

*If*, Polly reflected dizzily. Such a civilized term after so violent a loss of temper, brief though it had been. And she had discovered another double standard. The man who would be owned by no woman fully believed he owned his wife like a possession. But, ironically, what troubled her most at that instant was the stark awareness that she had really upset Raul. Yet she hadn't a clue why her silly sarcastic comments should have exploded his cool, controlled façade into a shocking blaze of primitive fury.

'Put it down to jet lag,' Raul added almost jerkily, pushing long brown fingers restively through his glossy blueblack hair. 'You are not *that* kind of woman. If you had been, I would never have agreed to marry you.'

What kind of woman? The unfaithful type? What a peculiar thought for a male like Raul to harbour! For, on the face of it, Raul Zaforteza was a real heartbreaker, possessed of every quality most likely to hold a woman's attention. Personality, looks, sex-appeal, wealth, power. How many women would risk losing Raul by betraying him in another man's bed?

'I will join you at the ranch in a couple of days,' Raul murmured flatly as he moved past her—suddenly, she registered, keen to abandon the dialogue...and *her*? The suspicion hurt.

'Join me?' Polly echoed uncertainly. 'What are you talking about? Where are you going?'

'Tonight I'm afraid I'll have to stay in Caracas. Tomorrow I'll be in Maracaibo, and possibly the next day as well. I have several urgent business matters to deal with. I've been abroad for many weeks,' he reminded her drily.

Alone again, Polly freshened up and slid with a distinct lack of enthusiasm into the simple white cotton dress. When she returned to the main cabin she could not avoid noticing Irena's frequent starstruck glances in Raul's direction, and her pronounced need to hover at his elbow as eager as a harem slave to satisfy his every wish. No longer did she marvel at her own suspicions earlier. The brunette had a real giant-sized crush on Raul. And possibly Raul was so accustomed to inviting female flattery and exaggerated attention that he genuinely hadn't noticed.

'OK, so there *is* a problem,' Raul breathed, disconcerting Polly with a dark satiric glance of acknowledgement in Irena's direction while she was gathering up Luis's scattered possessions at the far end of the cabin. 'We were both fifty per cent wrong, but, believe me, I have never given her the slightest encouragement.'

Polly nodded in embarrassed silence, feeling like an idiot over the fuss she had made but fearful of re-opening the subject lest she make things even worse.

Raul parted from her at the airport as coolly and politely as a distant acquaintance, a shuttered look in his brilliant dark eyes. Irena escorted Polly onto the light plane which would whisk her and her son out to the Zaforteza ranch. Polly's heart was already sinking.

Would it always be like this with Raul? Would she never *know* Raul? Would she never understand what went on inside that complex and clever head of his? And was it possible that that 'urgent business' he had mentioned had merely been a convenient excuse to leave her? How humiliating it was to suspect that Raul *had* actually intended to accompany her to his home until she'd treated him to that foolish scene! After all, hadn't he told her up front that jealousy disgusted him, and that nothing would drive him away quicker?

It was lashing with rain when Polly clambered off the plane, protected by a giant umbrella extended over her and

Luis by the pilot. He helped her into the waiting four-wheel drive. Neither he nor the driver appeared to have a word of English. Polly was now feeling less guilty and more angry with Raul. How did he think it felt for her to arrive at the *estancia* alone, where nobody knew her and where very possibly nobody would even be able to speak to her?

Through the streaming windows she caught glimpses of a large spreading collection of buildings. Palm trees were being battered in the torrential downpour. And yet the heat was intense, the humidity high. A hellhole, Polly decided, in the right mood to make that snap judgement. Raul had posted them out to the boonies to live in a hellhole and just gone on his own sweet way, just as he was used to doing, just as he no doubt expected to *continue* doing...

A huge colonial-style house adorned by fancy verandahs and an upper balcony wreathed with climbers loomed out of the rain. Clutching Luis like a parcel, Polly made a dive through the torrent when the car door opened, fled up the steps and surged indoors into the mercifully air-conditioned cool without a single sidewise glance or pause.

She had a split second to catch her breath on the magnificence of the vast reception hall she stood in before she focused on the huddle of female servants sheltering behind the front door, all staring at her and the baby she held wide-eyed. Silence hung for the space of twenty seconds.

A tall and stunningly beautiful blonde strolled into view. Frowning regally at Polly, she shot something at her in Spanish.

'I'm sorry, I don't speak—'

'I am the Condesa Melina D'Agnolo. Where is Raul?' the woman demanded in accented but perfect English.

'Still in Caracas.' Conscious of the staff now sidling out of a door to the left as fast as mice escaping a cat, Polly gazed enquiringly at the other woman. Sheathed in a superb cerise suit, glittering jewellery adding to her imperious air of well-bred exclusivity, the lady exuded angry impatience.

'*Caracas?*' It was an infuriated shriek of disappointment.

As the shrill sound echoed off the high ceiling, Luis jerked in fright and let out a loud, fretful wail.

Melina D'Agnolo stalked forward and surveyed him with unconcealed distaste. 'So this is the child I have heard rumours about. It *does* exist. Well, what are you waiting for? Stop it making that horrible noise!'

'He's just hungry—'

'When will Raul arrive?'

'In a couple of days.'

'Then I shall wait for him,' Melina announced, eyes hardening as Luis continued to cry noisily in spite of Polly's efforts to console him. 'But you will keep that child upstairs, out of my sight and hearing.'

'I'm afraid I have no intention—' Polly began angrily.

'I will not tolerate impertinence. You will do as you are told or you will very soon find yourself out of a job!' Melina informed her. 'In Raul's absence, I am in charge here.'

Realising that she had been mistaken for an employee, Polly raised her head high, intending to explain that she was Raul's wife. But the other woman had already walked away to utter a sharp command in Spanish. A middle-aged woman in a black dress appeared so quickly she must have been waiting somewhere nearby. Melina issued what sounded like a staccato stream of instructions.

The older woman glanced in open dismay at Polly.

'The housekeeper will take you upstairs to the nursery. You can eat up there. I don't want to be bothered by the child...is that understood?'

'Why do you say you're in charge here? Are you related to Raul?' Polly enquired stiffly, and stood her ground.

Melina's green eyes narrowed with suggestive languor, full lips pouting into a coolly amused smile. 'I've never been asked to identify myself in this house before. Raul and I have been intimate friends for a very long time.'

Every scrap of colour drained from Polly's face. There was no mistaking the meaning of that proud declaration.

Her stomach curdled. It was a judgement on her, Polly thought sickly. She had foolishly made that scene over the infatuated Irena and now fate had served up her punishment: she was being confronted by the real thing. A genuine rival...

'Why are you looking at me like that?' Melina D'Agnolo enquired haughtily.

'I think this is going to be embarrassing,' Polly muttered.

Melina dealt her an impatient frown of incomprehension.

'Raul and I got married a month ago.'

The thunderous silence seemed to reverberate in Polly's ears, and then Luis started crying again.

The svelte blonde stared at Polly with raised brows, her incredulity unfeigned. 'It isn't possible that you are *married* to Raul—'

'I'm afraid it is...' Polly cut in, and switched her attention ruefully to the housekeeper still waiting for her.

The older woman murmured gently, 'Let me take the little one upstairs and feed him for you, *señora*.'

Grateful for the chance to remove Luis from the hostile atmosphere, Polly laid her son in the housekeeper's arms with a strained smile.

'*Señora?*' Melina D'Agnolo echoed the designation with stinging scorn. 'I think we need to talk.'

Raul, where are you when I need you? Polly thought in furious discomfiture. This was his department, not hers! How could Raul possibly have overlooked the necessity of telling his mistress that he had acquired a wife? Polly turned reluctantly back to face the angry blonde. 'I don't think that would be a good idea.'

'If you prefer it, we can talk out here, where all the staff can hear us.'

Rigid with tension, Polly followed Melina into a gracious reception room filled with superb antique furniture. 'I don't see that we *have* anything to say to each other—'

'Obviously Raul married you because of the child. The oldest ploy of all. I expect you think you've been very clever.' Melina loosed a grim little laugh. 'Yes, I'm shocked, and I don't mind admitting it. Ten years ago Raul loved me, but he *still* wouldn't marry me, so I married someone else to teach him a lesson!'

Wanting no share of such confidences, Polly hovered, stiff with strain.

'So you needn't tell me that Raul loves you because I wouldn't believe it! I am the *only* woman Raul has ever loved,' Melina informed her with blistering confidence. 'I have never been concerned by his other little flirtations.'

'That's your business, not mine.'

'Your marriage won't last six months,' Melina said with dismissive certainty. 'Raul cherishes his freedom. When my husband died, I chose to be patient. I have never interfered with Raul's life—'

'Then don't do it now,' Polly slotted in tightly.

'If you think that is a possibility, you're even more of a child than you look!' Melina threw her a scornful look of superiority. 'And next month you'll be expected to deal with two hundred guests over the fiesta weekend. There'll be a rodeo, a friendly polo match and a non-stop party. Are you used to mixing with the wealthy élite? How good are you on a horse? I'm usually Raul's hostess, but now the job's yours...and if it doesn't go like clockwork, he'll be furious.'

Polly had paled. 'I'm sure I'll manage—'

'Raul will come back to me...of course he will. It's only a matter of time,' Melina asserted with contemptuous green eyes. 'If you're out of your depth with me, how much more out of your depth are you with him? I almost feel sorry for you. When Raul's bored, he is cruel and critical and callous—'

'I think it's time you left,' Polly interrupted flatly.

'If I were you, I wouldn't mention this meeting,' the blonde murmured sweetly as she strolled to the door. 'Raul detests jealous scenes. It would be much wiser for you to pretend that this meeting never took place.'

'Why should you be kind enough to give me that warning?'

Melina laughed unpleasantly. 'You already have all the problems you can handle. I shall enjoy watching you struggle to fill my shoes!'

Polly watched the blonde stalk across the hall and up the imposing staircase. She released her breath very slowly but she still felt utterly stunned. Melina D'Agnolo had been a severe shock. Raul's mistress—proud and unashamed of her position in his life and in no hurry to vacate his bed.

And one look at Melina had been sufficient to tell Polly that her misapprehension about the pretty stewardess on board the jet had been laughable. Melina was much more convincing in the role of mistress. Melina with her exquisite face, fabulous figure and tremendous elegance and poise. Mature, classy and sophisticated. Raul's kind of woman. And what even the greatest optimist would acknowledge as *seriously* challenging competition…

*No,* Polly scolded herself fiercely. She wasn't going to allow herself to start thinking that way. Raul had said that she was the only woman in his life now, and he had given her no cause to doubt his sincerity. OK, she had just suffered through a horribly embarrassing encounter and been forced to endure the other woman's spiteful attacks, but Melina would pack and depart and she would never have to see her again. She would put Melina right back out of her mind. Raul's past was none of her business, she reminded herself staunchly.

Upstairs, Polly wandered across a huge landing and picked a passageway. Finally, after a couple of wrong choices, she peered into a nursery as exquisitely furnished as a room in a glossy magazine. A crowd of smiling, whispering female staff surrounded the imposing antique four-poster cot. Freshly clothed and clearly content, Luis nestled within the cot's hand-embroidered bedding like a little king, giving an audience and basking in all the attention.

'It has been so long since there was a child here,' the housekeeper confided.

'Was this Raul's cot?' Polly asked, smiling.

The older woman looked away uncomfortably. 'No, *señora*...but it was his father's.'

Briefly wondering what she had said to disconcert the woman, Polly was led down a corridor lined with fabulous oil paintings and into a magnificent big bedroom. Realising that it had stopped raining, Polly opened the French windows and stepped out onto the sun-drenched balcony to gaze out appreciatively on the beautifully landscaped gardens. Lush lawns and colourful vegetation were shaded by clumps of graceful mature trees. In the distance an architectural extravaganza of a small building complete with turrets caught her attention.

'What's that used for?' she asked her companion.

The older woman stiffened. 'It is not used for anything, *señora*.'

'What a waste...it's so pretty.'

'It is full of ghosts, not a good place.' The housekeeper retreated back indoors, seemingly unaware that she had said anything that might cause Polly to stare after her in wide-eyed surprise and curiosity. 'I will fix you some breakfast, *señora*. You must be hungry.'

That evening, Polly rested back in the huge sunken bath in the *en suite* bathroom and felt like a queen lying in solitary state. She poked a set of pink toes up through the bubbles covering the surface of the water and sighed.

Melina D'Agnolo had vanished like the bad fairy. Only when she had disappeared had it occurred to Polly to wonder *how* she had gone, and to where. By car, by plane? The Zaforteza ranch was set in miles and miles of cattle country.

In the afternoon Polly had walked out to the furthest edge of the gardens and seen the plains stretching as far as the eye could reach in every direction, their monotony broken up by occasional clumps of trees, stretches of flood water that glinted in the hot sun and ground that seemed to sweep up and merge with the endless blue sky.

She closed her eyes and let herself think about Raul. Would he phone? Once she had told him not to bother and he hadn't given her a chance to say no a second time. But how the heck could she possibly measure up to a woman as gorgeous as Melina? The fear crept in and she tried to squash the thought and the feeling simultaneously.

'Lesson two on being a proper wife...' a silken drawl imparted lazily from the door. 'If you have to be in the bath when I come home, make it one I can share. Omit the heavily scented bubbles.'

# CHAPTER SEVEN

POLLY'S mouth fell open at the same instant as her eyes shot wide. Raul stood in the doorway, a sizzling smile of amusement slashing his mouth as he absorbed her astonishment.

'But you look kind of cute...' Raul conceded, brilliant dark eyes roaming with unconcealed interest over the rose-tipped breasts pertly breaking through the bubbles for his scrutiny.

Wrenching free of her paralysed stillness, Polly sat up in a frantic rush and hugged her knees to her chest. Raul gave an extravagant wince. 'Sometimes you act like a ten-year-old, *gatita.*'

'Couldn't you have knocked on the door?' Polly demanded defensively.

'The door wasn't even closed,' he reminded her drily, and he leant back against the door, slowly pushing it shut, as if he was making some kind of statement.

Sooner than ask him what he was doing, and already having discarded as too dangerously provocative the idea of asking him to step outside while she vacated the bath and covered herself, Polly studied him anxiously from below her dark lashes.

A tide of terrifying longing swept over her in a stormy wave. Her own heartbeat thundered inside her ears, and all the time her eyes were roaming all over him in hungry, helpless little darts. He was so incredibly tall in his light grey suit, his white shirt throwing his bronzed skin into exotic prominence, his luxuriant black hair gleaming under the recessed lights above, eyes glinting wicked gold in that lean, dark, devastating face.

'You missed me,' Raul purred, like a jungle cat basking in sunlight, his husky accent thickening and sending a trail of reaction down her taut spinal cord.

'For heaven's sake, how could I have missed you? I last saw you in the early hours of this morning!' Polly snapped, but it was a challenge to snap when it was so outrageously difficult to even breathe normally in his radius.

'You don't just need lessons on how to be a proper wife...you need a bloody intensive training course!' Raul shot back at her with shocking abruptness. 'What does it take to get a pleasant response from you? Thumbscrews?'

Jolted by that sudden blaze of temper, Polly gazed up at him strickenly. She felt the most awful stinging surge of tears threatening at the back of her eyes. Hurriedly she bent her head. Maybe meeting your gorgeous mistress spoilt my day, she almost slung accusingly, but caution restrained her.

'Maybe I'm not used to sharing a bathroom,' she muttered ruefully.

'Then this is where we will start,' Raul delivered.

Start what, where? Polly wondered in complete confusion.

'Dios...I can hardly believe I flew back here just to be with you!'

'Did you? I thought your urgent business took precedence.'

'Possibly the prospect of getting my bride horizontal on the marital bed had greater appeal.'

'Oh...' Polly said after a startled pause. 'Do you have to be so crude?'

Without the slightest warning, strong hands curved under her arms and a split second later she was airborne. Raul straightened and held her ruthlessly imprisoned in mid-air as she dripped water and bubbles everywhere, her shaken face aghast. 'Not so shrewish now, are you?' he murmured with unconcealed amusement.

'Please put me back in the water,' Polly mumbled pleadingly.

Raul gazed into her shrinking blue eyes and slowly lowered her back into the bath with careful hands. 'You're such a baby sometimes...I wasn't going to hurt you!' he breathed in stark reproach.

Still trembling, Polly hugged the far side of the bath. 'I don't know why I'm so nasty with you,' she lied—because she knew very well. 'I'm not usually like this with anybody.'

'You were so sweet in Vermont. I didn't even know you had a temper, never mind that viper's tongue,' Raul admitted wryly. 'What went wrong?'

*You did.* At that stupid question Polly was tempted to throw something at him. She had fallen hopelessly in love, more deeply in love than she had ever believed possible, and nothing had ever been the same since. He didn't love her, he didn't believe in love, and she couldn't risk letting him find out how she really felt about him. Given an ounce of such ego-boosting encouragement, he would walk all over her and take her for granted the way he had in Vermont.

The female sex had spoilt Raul. For minimum input he had always received maximum benefit—everything on his terms, everything the way *he* wanted it. And their marriage still felt like a deadweight threatening ball and chain to him. He didn't have to tell her that. She *knew* it. She marvelled that he should believe that taking her to bed would miraculously change anything, particularly when he had already spelt out the fact that he didn't rate sex any higher than an 'appetite'.

And where did that leave her? The virginal bride with novelty value? A fresh body for his enjoyment?

Raul discarded his jacket on a chair and tossed his tie on top of it. Emerging from her insecure reverie, Polly gaped. Shoes and socks were summarily discarded.

'What are you doing?'

Raul sent her a gleaming glance of intent. 'Losing your virginity is not akin to a visit to a sadistic dentist.'

'What would you know about it?'

A wolfish grin slashed his mobile mouth. 'I'll fill you in on my impressions tomorrow morning.'

Off came his shirt, to be carelessly discarded in a heap. Polly's throat clogged up at sight of that magnificent brown torso and the triangle of all male dark curling hair outlining his powerful pectoral muscles. 'Is this my anatomy lesson?' she whispered shakily.

'You need one?' As free of inhibition as she was repressed, Raul flicked loose his belt and slid out of his well-cut trousers.

Although Polly wanted to look away, she couldn't. Her throat thickened, her mouth running dry. Her mesmerised attention locked on to the silky furrow of hair running down over his flat, taut stomach to disappear tantalisingly beneath the band of a pair of black briefs.

'You're beginning to embarrass *me*,' Raul censured mockingly.

Caught staring, Polly twisted her head away, cheeks flaming. 'I don't think anything embarrasses you!' she condemned unevenly.

'You really *are* shy…I thought it was an act in Vermont,' Raul confessed without warning. 'You were so open and forthright in every other way—'

'I don't put on acts,' Polly protested feverishly. 'I can't help the way I was brought up any more than you can.'

'What's that supposed to mean?' Raul breathed with sudden brooding darkness.

Involuntarily she shivered, catching the warning nuances in his accented drawl and spooked by what she could not understand. 'My father believed girls should be modest and quiet and strait-laced, and my godmother agreed with him—'

'Whatever happened to the "quiet"?' Raul cut in with unhesitating humour.

Her momentary ripple of foreboding ebbed, only to be replaced by a more pressing urge to leap out of the bath as

Raul stepped in. Arms wrapped tightly round her knees, Polly twisted her head back round and slung him an accusing glance as he settled fluidly down on the other side of the bath and rested his burnished dark head back against the inset cushioning.

'Look, why can't we just do it in bed like other people?' she suddenly launched at him in mortified condemnation. 'I think you're going out of your way to make this more difficult for me!'

Dealing her a briefly bemused appraisal, Raul suddenly flung his head back and burst out laughing without restraint. *'Caramba, cielito—'*

'That is *it*...that is *finally* it!' Polly raked at him, chagrin tipping over into a sudden empowering rage that enabled her to begin rising without any constraining fear of exposing her own body.

Raul leant forward and caught her hand, tipping her sufficiently off-balance to ensure that she was powerless to resist the ease with which he reached up his other hand and tumbled her down on top of him, water splashing everywhere.

Panting furiously for breath, Polly pulled herself back from him. 'Let go of me!'

Raul regarded her with deceptive languor. 'I wasn't actually planning to consummate our marriage here...I just wanted to talk...'

'T-talk?' Polly parroted weakly as she subsided back beneath the water to conceal herself, carefully avoiding the slightest contact with his long extended limbs.

'No need to panic...at least...not yet,' Raul drawled smoothly, the golden gleam deep in his shimmering dark eyes increasing the colour in her hot face. 'In my innocence I believed that this was a comparatively mild first step towards greater intimacy.'

'Do you normally just *talk* in the bath with your women?' Polly practically snarled in her discomfiture, knowing that any plea of innocence was not to be trusted

in this instance, perfectly well aware that Raul was highly
amused by her enervated state.

The golden gleam vanished, leaving her gazing in sudden
fear into wintry cool dark eyes. '*Infierno!* You're obsessed.
Jealousy is a very destructive thing. Do you want to destroy
us before we even begin with these constant attacks?'

Pale now, Polly just closed her eyes. In the space of a
moment she saw a dozen beautiful female faces skim cruelly through her mind's eye. Only then did she grasp the
source of her jealousy, the day when it had been born to
increase the bitterness she had experienced after leaving
Vermont. To satisfy her driving need to know more about
the father of her child, she had gone to the library and
scanned through newspaper gossip pages and glossy society
magazines...

Time after time she had come on photos of Raul with
some gorgeous blonde babe on his arm. And that was the
day when she had finally accepted how pitiful her love was,
how hopelessly without foundation or any prospect of re-
ciprocation.

Then, months on, to have that impression of Raul as a
heartless womaniser reinforced all over again—to watch
Raul leave that London clinic to walk into another woman's
arms, to live through that mortifying misunderstanding
about the stewardess and then the very same day to be
confronted with the horrendous real shock of Melina
D'Agnolo. Was it any wonder that she was desperately insecure, afraid to trust Raul and lashing out in an attempt to
protect herself from further pain?

'I won't live like this with any woman,' Raul breathed
with terrifying quietness. 'It's like trying to fight an invisible enemy... Whatever I do you'll always be suspicious!'

As he pulled himself upright, her lashes lifted. Stepping
out of the bath, Raul snatched a fleecy towel from the rail
and strode back into the bedroom without a backward
glance.

And, just as suddenly, Polly's defensive attitude fell

away. She saw a marriage which hadn't even begun now going down the drain without fanfare. She saw the chance she had been given thrown away out of proud defiance and a refusal to face her own insecurities and faults.

Raul hadn't made love to her in Vermont. *She* had been the one who had misinterpreted *his* intentions. He had had the right to pursue other relationships. His freedom had been his own and she had had no claim on him. That was the reality which she had failed to accept all these months because *she* had fallen in love. And what was she doing now but driving Raul away from her, in spite of the fact that he had given her no cause to distrust him?

In a panic, now that she had seen herself at fault, Polly climbed out of the bath, tugged a black towelling robe off a wall hook and hurriedly dug her arms into the too long sleeves.

'Raul...I'm sorry!' she called in advance, afraid he might already have left the bedroom beyond.

'Forget it...I need some fresh air.'

Rolling up the sleeves of what she now realised had to be his robe, Polly edged apprehensively round the door and peered out. Damp black wildly tousled hair flopping over his bronzed brow, Raul was zipping up a pair of skintight cream jodhpurs.

In silence, she watched him yank highly polished leather boots out of a cupboard and sink down on the chaise longue at the foot of the bed to pull them on. 'You're going riding?' she muttered uncertainly. 'But it's getting dark.'

'Get back in your bath with your bubbles,' Raul advised with brooding satire. 'Immerse that little body you protect so assiduously...and leave me alone.'

'Look...I said I was sorry.' Polly lifted her chin. 'Do I have to crawl?'

Raul lifted his dark head and regarded her directly for the first time since she had entered the room. She was shaken by the black brooding distance etched with clarity in his spectacular dark eyes. 'How are you on disappearing?' he drawled in a tone like a silken whiplash. 'Because right now, I just don't want to be around you.'

Polly flinched from that brutal candour, the flush of pink in her cheeks receding to leave her paper-pale. Without warning, Raul was like a dark, intimidating stranger.

'So go back in the bathroom before I say anything else to hurt your sensitive feelings,' Raul told her harshly. 'I'm not in the mood to control my tongue!'

'I'm not afraid of what you have to say.'

'Then why the hell are you goading me like this?' Raul splintered back at her in frustration. 'I don't like being needled. I especially don't like snide comments. If you have something to say to me, have the guts to say it loud and clear, because I have no time for anything else!'

Melina loomed like the bad fairy in her mind's eye. Polly wanted to defend herself. She wanted to explain how upsetting and threatening she had found that encounter. But she had a greater fear that the mention of her own feelings in relation to yet another woman and him would be a dangerously provocative act that would simply send him through the roof. As he gazed expectantly back at her, Raul's eyes burned as gold as the flames in the heart of a fire.

'I haven't anything to say,' she stated, in what she hoped was a soothing tone likely to defuse the situation.

But, disconcertingly, that tone had the same effect as throwing paraffin on a bonfire. Raul sprang up, throwing her a blistering glance of derision. 'You have the backbone of a jellyfish! I'm ashamed to be married to such a spiritless excuse for a woman!'

'Maybe...m-maybe I have more control over my temper than you have,' Polly stammered through teeth clenched with restraint.

Raul slashed an imperious hand through the air in savage dismissal. 'This morning I left you at the airport. I walked away from conflict. I've spent the last ten years doing that quite happily. I watched my father do that all his life with

women,' he grated in a raw, hostile undertone. 'And then
it dawned on me that I was married to you, and that if I
start closing you out when you anger me, what future can
this marriage have?'

'Raul, I—'

'*Cállate!* I am talking,' Raul broke in with supreme contempt as he yanked a garment out of a drawer. 'I find your
continuing jealousy irrational and disturbing. And for
someone so repressed she shrinks from even sharing a bath
with her own husband, I find it even stranger that you
should want to know what I might or might not have done
with other women when I was answerable to nobody!'

Lips bloodlessly compressed to prevent them from trembling like the rest of her shivering, woefully weak body,
Polly watched him pull on a white polo shirt and whispered
shamefacedly. 'I don't want to know...' She was stumbling
wretchedly. 'I *mean*—'

'Never again will I make the smallest sacrifice to make
this marriage work!' Raul swore with hard emphasis. 'I
have my son...what else do I need? Certainly not a silly
little girl who cowers at the idea of making love with me!'

'Raul, please...' Polly muttered strickenly as he strode
towards the door and flung it wide.

All volatile energy and movement now, he yelled something down the corridor. On cottonwool legs, Polly followed him to the threshold and watched one of the maids
coming at an anxious run.

Raul rapped out instructions in Spanish. The maid
bobbed her head in instant acquiescence and then sped off
down the corridor again.

Raul sent Polly a smouldering look of derision. 'You
need no longer fear my unwelcome approaches, *mi esposa*.
The maid will convey your possessions to another room!'

# CHAPTER EIGHT

POLLY paced the floor in the beautiful guest room the housekeeper had allotted to her without once meeting her eyes. The shame of so new a bride being ejected from the marital bedroom had been fully felt on Polly's behalf.

Over the next couple of hours, Polly ran the gamut of fiercer emotions than she had ever known. She had never come across anyone with a temper as volatile as Raul's. She had never dreamt that Raul might speak to her like that—even worse, *look* at her as he had. As if she was nothing to him, less than nothing, even, nothing but a pain and a nuisance, beneath his notice and utterly unworthy of any further attention.

She went from rage at his having made such a public spectacle of their differences to sudden all-engulfing pain at the sheer strength of that rejection. They had been together perhaps twenty-four hours, yet everything had fallen apart. A voice in her mind just screamed that she couldn't cope, couldn't handle the situation. She wanted to take Luis and run...run and make Raul *sorry*, she registered. The tears flowed then, in shame at the manner in which her thoughts went round and round in circles but never lost the need to keep Raul at the very centre.

Calmer, if no more happy once she had cried, she took a good, hard look at her own behaviour and didn't like what she saw. And when she exerted herself to try and see things from Raul's point of view, she just groaned and squirmed at her own foolish prickly resentment and insecurity.

Gorgeous, woman-killing, much sought-after and fêted guy becomes unwilling husband but makes decent effort to paper over the cracks. What with? Sex. What else? He doesn't *know* anything else. Every other woman can't wait to get him between the sheets to check out that fabled reputation, but his bride is inexplicably and therefore offensively reluctant. Not only reluctant but also sarcastic, jealous, and seemingly incapable of behaving like a mature adult committed to getting their marriage of convenience up and running.

And why had she behaved like an idiot?

Because she loved him, Polly conceded painfully, and she wanted, needed to be so much more than a convenient body in Raul's bed. And, worst of all, a sexually ignorant partner when he had to be accustomed to lovers with a considerable degree of sophistication and expertise, not to mention lithe and perfect bodies. So, out of stubborn pride and resentment over her own sense of inadequacy, she had driven him away.

If she had told him straight off about that clash with Melina D'Agnolo, at least he would have understood why she was in such a prickly mood. But she had missed her opportunity and knew that it would be an act of insanity to risk opening such a subject with Raul now. In fact even the thumbscrews he had mentioned wouldn't dredge Melina's name from her lips...not when he already saw her as an obsessively jealous woman.

And all his self-preserving male antennae were in perfect working order, Polly acknowledged at the lowest ebb of self-honesty. She was and had been jealous, and no doubt would be jealous again, because jealousy thrived on insecurity. And she *did* want to own Raul, body and soul.

Seeing how swollen her eyes were in the mirror, she splashed her face over and over again with cold water. Then she washed her hair, put on a little light make-up, some perfume and slid into one of the silk nighties he had given her. Creeping down the corridor like a burglar sneaking under the cover of darkness, she walked back into the marital bedroom and clambered into the big wide bed to watch the moonlight slant across the ceiling through the undrawn curtains.

She must have fallen asleep, because she woke with a start later, hearing running feet and then raised anxious voices in the corridor outside. Thrusting her tumbled hair off her sleepy face, she switched on the light and lurched out of bed. Opening the bedroom door, she peered out.

A clutch of gesticulating staff surrounded Raul. Liberally daubed in mud, and far from his usual immaculate self, he looked frantic, shooting out questions at volume, expressive hands moving at volatile speed to indicate his level of angry concern.

'Raul…?' Polly called worriedly as he paused for breath. 'What's wrong?'

The staff huddle twisted round with a general look of astonishment.

'Where the hell have you been?' Raul thundered at her accusingly.

'In bed…sleeping,' Polly mumbled in bewilderment. 'Why?'

'*Why?*' Raul roared back in apparent disbelief.

The staff were now all slowly rolling back like a quiet tide in the direction of the stairs. Raul strode past her into the bedroom, shooting the rumpled bed a speaking glance of seeming amazement.

'Lesson three on being a proper wife.' Polly whispered her prepared opening sentence before she could lose her nerve. 'Never let the sun go down on a row.'

'It's rising…the sun,' Raul informed her half under his breath and, bending down, he scooped her unresisting body up into his arms, crossed the room and settled her back on the bed.

Frowning, not following that oddly strained if true remark, as the dawn light was indeed already burnishing the night sky, Polly gazed uncertainly up at him. 'What was going on out there?'

Dark colour flared over his superb cheekbones and his

wide, sensual mouth hardened. 'You weren't where you were supposed to be. I thought you'd bolted again.'

'B-bolted where?' Polly asked, with some difficulty squashing the incautious giggle trying to break free of her taut throat.

'How do I know? There's two helicopters out there, a whole collection of cars, a stable full of horses! If you wanted to bolt, it wouldn't be much of a challenge to find the means,' Raul informed her grimly as he stood over her, six foot plus of dark, menacing authority. 'My bed was the last place I expected to find you!'

So he hadn't even looked. He had jumped to conclusions. He had checked the bedroom she should have been in and immediately raised the alarm. Although she was deeply embarrassed by that candid admission that he hadn't dreamt she would have the nerve to take up residence in his bed, she was also rather relieved to register that Raul was not omnipotent. He could not yet forecast her every move. But she turned her head away from the light, fearful that he would see too much in her expressive face.

'Do you want me to go?' she asked with studied casualness.

'No...I can recognise an olive tree when I'm handed one.'

'You mean an olive *branch*,' she contradicted gently.

'No, when you put on silk, scent, mascara and lipstick for my benefit, and arrange yourself like a little bridal sacrifice in my bed...' Raul murmured almost roughly as he stared down at her, brilliant eyes reflecting only the light in his darkly handsome features '...it's definitely not just a branch, it's a whole tree...in fact, it might well be the equivalent of an orchard.' He thrust impatient fingers through his disordered hair and shook his head ruefully. '*Dios mío*...what am I talking about?'

Standing there, talking like that, he seemed disturbingly different. He was still regarding her with a piercing, narrow-eyed intensity that didn't seem to be making him any

more comfortable than it was making her. In fact, he looked
pretty pale beneath his healthy bronze skin. As Polly was
already achingly self-conscious about lying there in his bed,
his reactions were increasing her anxiety level. Here she
was, offering an invitation to the best of her ability, but
maybe he no longer even *wanted* that invitation!

The tense silence seemed to scream in her ears.

'You must've been out riding for a long time...' she
commented, desperate to break that nerve-straining quiet.

'I went some distance. I called in with...with a neighbour.' His stubborn jawline clenched, handsome mouth
compressing, strong face suddenly shadowing as he strode
towards the bathroom. 'I'm filthy. I need a shower.'

Pink-cheeked now, Polly studied him the same way a
crossword addict without talent studies the *crème de la
crème* of challenges, desperate for a hint of true inspiration.
He stepped out of view, and she listened then to the
strangely intimate sounds of a man undressing: the thud of
his boots hitting the tiled floor, the snap as he presumably
undid the waistband of his jodhpurs...

Oh, dear heaven, if Raul no longer even wanted her to
share his bed, how did she get out of this situation without
losing face?

'Maybe I should go back to my room,' Polly practically
whispered.

Sudden silence fell.

Bare-chested and barefoot, Raul appeared in the doorway, all rampant virility with rumpled hair and the jodhpurs
which had an indecently faithful fit to his long, lean thighs
undone at his waist. 'Whatever you feel most comfortable
doing.'

On receipt of that refusal to state an opinion either way—
which from a male of Raul's domineering temperament was
particularly hard to take—Polly blinked in bemused chagrin.

'But you can sleep here just as easily,' Raul pointed out
with a careless shrug.

'Fine…' Polly managed to splutter, turning over on her side to glower with stinging eyes at the dawn filling the sky with such vibrant colour. The unfeeling louse didn't *want* an orchard of olive branches. Her so sophisticated, sexy and immensely self-assured husband was trying to let her down gently. And now she was stuck, because if she jumped out of bed and fled she was going to look really stupid and pathetic! And, furthermore, Raul would then work out for himself that her olive branch had been rather more emotionally motivated than she'd chosen to admit.

She listened to the shower switching off and grimaced. The lights went out. The mattress gave at the other side of the bed.

'If you sleep any closer to the edge, you might fall out,' Raul remarked lazily.

'I don't want to get in your way!' Polly snapped childishly.

Raul released his breath in an audible hiss. 'You don't have anything to fear, *gatita*. I realise that I've been…inconsiderate,' he selected after an uncharacteristic hesitation.

Stiff as a board, Polly strove to work out the intent of that unexpected admission.

'Naturally I want you to be happy,' Raul informed her out of the blue.

'Do you?'

'Of course. Why so amazed?' Raul queried. 'What else would I want?'

'You want the best for Luis,' Polly breathed, not quite levelly. 'I understand that—'

'*Dios*…when I thought you'd gone I never even thought to check on our son!' His slightly dazed tone was that of a male belatedly making that connection and not best pleased by it.

Good heavens, Polly thought in shock over that astonishing admission. Raul had actually thought of *her* first, put *her* first? Instantly it was as if a tight little knot of resentment was jerked loose inside her. She no longer felt like an unwanted wife, to be tolerated only because their son needed his mother. And she wondered when Raul's single-minded focus on Luis had stretched to include her as a person of some import in his own life. But she really didn't care *when* that minor miracle had taken place, she was just so very grateful that it had.

'I wouldn't bolt again…as you put it,' she shared awkwardly.

'I can forgive you for Vermont. That was understandable. The clinic too…you panicked. That's all in the past now.'

Polly turned over. 'But coming here was still a big thing for me…'

'No less a challenge for me, *querida*.' Raul reached for her clenched fingers where they lay above the sheet, and calmly tugged her across the divide between them.

Her breath caught in her throat as he eased her into his arms. Gazing up at him, she drank in the hard bones forming that lean, strong face, her stomach fluttering, her heartbeat racing, every fibre of her body pitched in anticipation of his next move.

Raul rubbed a blunt forefinger gently over the ripe fullness of her parted lips and looked down at her. A sigh feathered in her throat, her eyes widening, dark blue pools of unconscious invitation. 'I…I was just nervous earlier,' she confided.

'You have beautiful eyes. That was the first thing I ever noticed about you.'

'In Vermont?'

'I saw you long before then.'

Her brow furrowed. 'But *how*?'

'Your photograph, then your initial interview with my lawyer. Trick mirror. I was in the office next door,' he confided without apology.

'Devious,' she said breathlessly, her heart hammering as she stared up into mesmeric golden eyes.

'Cautious,' Raul contradicted.

The hard heat of his lean, virile body was seeping into her by pervasive degrees. She was so outrageously conscious of his proximity that she was keeping her lungs going on tiny little pants. 'Kiss me,' she muttered, before she could lose her nerve.

'I'm burning up to possess you,' Raul breathed thickly. 'I won't stop at kissing.'

She trembled and, closing her eyes, reached up to press her lips against his. Teasingly he circled her mouth with his own, refusing to deepen the pressure, and in sudden driving impatience Polly sank her fingers into the depths of his luxuriant black hair to pull him down to her.

Vibrant amusement shimmered in his eyes as he held himself above her. 'Is that a yes?'

Shaken then by her own boldness, she met the reckless golden glitter of sensual threat in his gaze and started melting down deep inside, the weighted languor of anticipation sentencing her to stillness. Helplessly she nodded.

With a slashing smile that turned her heart over, Raul lowered his imperious dark head. 'You have to understand that this is a first for me too,' he shared silkily. 'I've never had a virgin in my bed. It makes you very special.'

'I never know whether you're being ironic or sincere,' Polly muttered tautly.

'Only a very stupid man would be ironic on his wedding night,' Raul asserted as he brought his hard, mobile mouth passionately down on hers.

He kissed her with innate eroticism, parting her lips, letting his tongue plunge deep into the honeyed warmth within, seeking out and finding every tender spot. Clutching at him, she was madly conscious of every slight movement he made, and wholly at the mercy of the wild, sweet, seductive feelings sweeping through her quivering body. It was a passionate, urgent exploration that betrayed his very masculine hunger, a growl of satisfaction escaping his throat before he lifted his head again, surveying her with shameless satisfaction.

'I told you that you would come to me, *mi esposa*.'

Her lashes fluttered up. She gave him a dazed look of reproach, too shaken by the effect he was having on her to muster a tart response. He came back to her again, tasting her, delving deep and then skimming the tender roof of her mouth in a flickering, provocative caress until she was gasping for breath but still hanging onto him.

Leaning back from her then, an unashamedly predatory smile on his sensual mouth, Raul trailed the ribbon straps of her nightgown slowly down over her slight shoulders, brushing them down her arms and then carefully slipping her hands free at the wrists.

'I want to look at all of you,' he breathed huskily. 'Touch all of you. Taste every smooth, silken inch of that pale, perfect skin and then sink so deep into you, you won't know where I end and you begin.'

Transfixed, and hectically flushed, Polly stared up at him, utterly overpowered by the tiny little tremors already racking her taut length, the tormenting throb of heat she could feel between her slender thighs. Torn between fascination and shyness, she watched him smoothly tug down the bodice of her nightgown so that her small, firm breasts sprang free, her nipples already wantonly distended rosy buds.

'Raul, please...' she moaned, hot with a debilitating and confusing mix of embarrassment and excitement.

'*Dios*...but you are exquisite.' His dark golden eyes blazed over her bare breasts with urgent appreciation and made her tremble.

With deft but impatient hands, Raul eased the nightgown tangled round her waist down over her slim hips, raising her knees to slide the garment finally free and discard it.

Smoothing a soothing hand over her shifting hips, he ran intent eyes over the slender length of her, her tiny waist, delicately rounded stomach, the cluster of dark curls crowning the juncture of her trembling thighs. As she made a sudden impulsive snatch at the sheet, he forestalled her, and gazed down at her with a wicked smile. 'I've waited a long time to see you like this.' Long brown fingers closed round her wrist and lingered. 'Your pulse is going crazy. Admit it…it's exciting to be looked at, appreciated and lusted over. What did you expect, *querida*? That I would fall on you like a clumsy, selfish boy and it would all be over in minutes? That is not how I make love…'

'No…' Polly conceded shakily, scarcely able to swallow, so constricted was her throat.

A dark line of colour lay over his superb cheekbones. 'I want this to be good for you…I want you to spend all day aching for the moment when I take you in my arms again…'

Trembling like a leaf, with the heat surging through her in waves, Polly mumbled, 'Ambitious…'

'Always…in everything. It's in my blood,' Raul husked in agreement, running an exploring hand lightly over her outrageously sensitive breasts and forcing a gasp of startled reaction from her.

Helplessly she strained up to him, and with the tip of his tongue he provocatively traced the already reddened curve of her lips, so that she tipped her head back, openly inviting the hot, hard pressure of his mouth which every sense craved.

With a roughened laugh he tasted her again, sliding a hand beneath her hips and pressing her into contact with the aggressive thrust of his own arousal, and excitement drenched her in a blinding, burning wave. She moaned beneath that devastating mouth of his, need rising like a greedy fire as he let his fingers finally stroke and tug her achingly sensitive nipples. Freeing her swollen lips, he slid down the bed and employed that expert mouth on her tender breasts instead.

Pushing up against him, she twisted wildly, unprepared for the raw tide of sensation engulfing her now. Every intimate caress felt so unbearably good, yet all the time she strained and yearned helplessly for more, intoxicated by physical feelings she had never experienced before and ruled by their demands.

'Easy, *gatita*,' Raul muttered softly, pulling her to him, stilling her helpless squirmings with the momentary weight of one long, powerful thigh. 'We're not running a race...'

Polly snatched in a long, shuddering breath, focusing on him in a dazed kind of wonderment. 'I didn't know it would be like this...'

'Like a raging fire in which two can burn up with pleasure?' Raul bent over her and let his lips brush tenderly over hers.

She jerked as he eased her thighs apart and embarked on a more intimate invasion, touching her where she had never been touched before, discovering the damp silken ache at the centre of her. And he caressed her with such shrewd comprehension of what would excite her most that she was overwhelmed by the uncontrollable pleasure, sobbing against his broad shoulder, always longing and needing and finally begging for more as the desperate need for greater fulfilment rose to screaming proportions inside her.

And then Raul came smoothly over her, and surged into her before she could even get the chance to fear the unknown. As he thrust deeper there was a short, sharp pain that made her cry out, and then, a split second later, the most extraordinary and intense feeling of physical pleasure as he abruptly stilled to gaze with rather touching anxiety down at her.

'I hoped it wouldn't hurt,' Raul confessed raggedly.

And Polly smiled a little dizzily up at him, at that moment loving him so much for caring that she was weak with the strength of the emotion shrilling through her.

'Doesn't matter,' she swore unsteadily.

And then he moved within her again, and her eyes slid shut on the rush of sensation which was so indescribably seductive and controlling. If he had stopped she would have died, and she wrapped herself round him, utterly lost within the surging domination of his possession. He drove her up to the heights and she splintered there in ecstasy, glorying in his groan of intense physical pleasure as he slammed into her one last time with compulsive driving force.

Eyes welling with tears from the sheer raw intensity of her emotions, Polly held him tight within the circle of her arms, revelling in the sweetness of her new right to do that, openly and unashamedly, without fear of revealing too much. And she marvelled at how much closer she felt to Raul now. She wanted those timeless, tranquil moments to last for ever. He was an absolutely fantastic lover, she decided. Lying in that gloriously intimate embrace and knowing that she had satisfied him, in spite of her inexperience, filled her with new pride and confidence.

In that same instant of heady contentment Raul pulled away from her and sprawled back against the pillows again. He flipped his tousled dark head over and surveyed her with deceptively indolent dark golden eyes that gleamed with satisfaction. 'You see, love isn't necessary to sexual gratification.'

Already hurt by the speed of his withdrawal from physical proximity, Polly gazed back at him with a sinking sensation in her stomach. 'Is there a point to that comment?' she asked tautly.

'I think you get the point.'

'It's a re-run of the "don't expect too much from me," escape hatch for the commitment-shy male, is it?' Polly condemned on a rush of bitter pain that filled her with a furious need to strike back. 'You are just so terrified of emotion I actually feel sorry for you, but why should you worry about disappointing me? After all, you've been disappointing me one way or another ever since the first day we met!'

Stunned by that ringing and unexpected indictment, any pretense of indolence now abandoned, Raul stared at her, eyes dangerous as black ice. 'Is that a fact?' he breathed unevenly—only so thick was his accent it sounded much more like, 'Ees-zat-a-fat?', so she knew she had hit home very hard.

Polly snatched up her nightie and pulled it over her head with trembling hands. 'Yes...but it hardly matters,' she assured him with a skimming look of scorn. 'I have nothing to lose and I'm not lowering my needs to the level of yours. You're on probation, Raul.'

So incensed was he by that patronising little speech, he threw back the sheet and sprang out of bed. 'I...Raul Zaforteza...on *probation*?' he gritted in savage disbelief.

Squaring her slight shoulders, Polly was unrepentant. 'And so far you are not doing very well. You seem to think you've done me one very big favour marrying me...but ask me how *I* feel five months from now—'

'*Por qué?* What the hell is going to happen in five months?' Raul raked at her across the depth of the bedroom.

'I will inherit my godmother's money, and if I'm not happy with you, I'm not spending the rest of my life in misery.'

'*Misery?*' Raul ground out in outrage.

'I'm not,' Polly told him, and meant it. 'You needn't think you can toss diamond jewellery at me to keep me happy. Diamonds are quite pretty, but not something I feel I have to have.'

'*Pretty?*' Raul echoed in rampant disbelief.

'Other things mean much more to me...respect, affection, caring. I do appreciate that you have probably spent the entirety of your adult life giving extravagant gifts to women because you can't cope with emotional demands, but—'

'How dare you say I cannot cope?' Volatile golden eyes slammed into hers in a look as hostile as a physical assault.

'You said it yourself. You said you walk away when things get difficult.' Polly made that incendiary reminder with reluctance.

Raul studied her with a seething, wordless incomprehension that twisted her heart inside out. Then he spun away, presenting her with the long golden sweep of his flawless back to wrench open a drawer and start to haul on a pair of black jeans. She knew he didn't even trust himself to speak. She knew he was infuriated by the sudden struggle speaking English had become because he was in such an ungovernable rage.

'I realize I'm far from perfect, and that a lot of things I do and say must irritate you...but I don't think I deserve to feel that you only came home tonight to have sex with me,' Polly told him, her eyes stinging so hard she had to open her eyes very wide to hold the tears back. 'Like I'm some sort of novelty act...and then, right after it, regardless of my feelings, you have to gloat—'

On that charge, Raul swung back. 'All I said was that love was not necessary to—'

Polly drew in a deep, shuddering breath. 'And why did you say that?' she whispered painfully, suddenly sick and tired of pretending. 'You knew it wasn't true. You *must* know how I feel about you. I think you've *always* known...'

Raul went very still. Dense black lashes dropped low, spectacular eyes betraying only a glint of gold, ferocious tension tightening his bronzed skin over his fabulous bone structure. 'You're going to regret this...'

'No, I won't. I'm past caring,' Polly muttered with perfect truth. 'I love you to death, and you probably knew it before I did! If you'd had a single shred of decency you would've backed off in Vermont. In the same way you knew exactly why I wanted to marry you...yet you told Digby I was a gold-digger and a blackmailer. It's like a big black secret you won't acknowledge, but I won't live a lie, Raul.'

Utterly drained by that stark baring of her own tormented emotions, Polly slid out of the bed and walked towards the door.

'*Dios*…I can't give you love!' Raul launched at her with positive savagery.

'But with a little effort you could make a reasonable stab at respect, if not anything else. Because if you don't,' Polly whispered jaggedly, torn in two with pain and the regret he had so accurately forecast she would feel, 'I'll stop loving you, and love is all you have to hold me. I won't be a doormat…I won't be walked on.'

Without looking back, she flipped the door shut behind her. She was in a complete daze, shock at what she had done and said hitting her all at once. She was shaking all over, moving towards the sanctuary of the guest room she had abandoned earlier on jellied knees. But somehow she didn't feel like crying any more. What had passed between her and Raul had been too devastating. A shame something she had found so wonderful, so beautiful, had had to end in such emotional agony.

Raul simply couldn't have allowed it to stay that good. He had had to open that smart mouth of his and blow everything apart. Make her feel like a one-night stand instead of a wife who loved him—and who he knew damned well loved him! In the clear dawn light she lay down on the bed, a giant, aching hole where her heart had been. She didn't want a heart that hurt her so much.

When the door opened again, she sat up with a start. Raul thrust the door shut behind him and studied her, brilliant black eyes incisive.

'I too have faults,' Raul murmured. 'But, unlike you, I acknowledge them.'

'What are you saying?' Feeling worn and drained, Polly simply bowed her head defensively over her raised knees.

'Yes, I disappointed you in Vermont…but then you disappointed me too.'

Disconcerted by that assurance, Polly lifted her head. Raul held her questioning look with unflinching cool.

'If you had been the truly honest woman you like to believe you are, you would have told me that you were pregnant then. But, when it suited your purposes to remain silent, you were as neglectful of the truth as I was about my real identity. I think we're about equal on the score of disappointing each other,' Raul completed drily.

A slow, painful pink had surged into Polly's cheeks. It shook her to be faced with the fact that she had also made mistakes—not least by ignoring reality when it seemed to be within her own interests to do so. She had never come close to telling Raul that she was a surrogate mum-to-be, had been too frightened he would reject her in disgust. How ironic it was that he had known all along, and even judged her on that cowardly silence!

'I suppose you're right,' she contrived to force out rather hoarsely.

'As for last night, and your conviction that I only returned to have sex with you—do you really think I am so immature *or* so desperate for sexual release?' At that searing demand, Polly twisted her head away, no longer caring how he translated such a reaction. 'I'm here now because I accepted that I shouldn't have left you in the first place, and that such behaviour would only reinforce your fears about our future.'

Polly linked her fingers fiercely tight together. All rage put behind him, Raul's ice-cool and rational rebuttal of her angry accusations was a cruelly effective weapon of humiliation. 'OK,' she got out, when she couldn't bear his expectant silence any longer.

'And do you really think that threatening to leave me in five months' time is likely to add to the stability of our marriage?'

Polly flinched as if he had cracked a whip over her. She felt like a child being told off for bad behaviour.

'Now I think you're going to sulk,' Raul forecast, with an even more lowering air of adult restraint.

Polly struggled, and finally managed to swallow the enormous lump in her throat. 'I think you're probably right.'

# CHAPTER NINE

RAUL's equestrian centre was a vastly impressive installation set about a mile from the ranch. Polly settled Luis into his stroller and wandered down the asphalt lane in the sweltering heat, striving not to look like a woman out in search of her husband. But the truth was she was getting desperate, for she had seen virtually nothing of Raul over the past few days.

Indeed, after those twin earth-shattering scenes at dawn, she had initially expected to find Raul a good thousand miles away on business by the time he appeared the following day. Why? Because he was thoroughly fed up with her! Fed up with the virtual minefield she had already made of their marriage of convenience and fed up with her over-emotional reactions. What had happened to patience? Calm? Reasoned restraint?

But in the cruellest possible way she had Raul trapped. He might not be able to respond to emotional demands, but, challenged with an accusation of cowardice, sheer horror that she might be right would keep him on the spot. Only 'on the spot' at the ranch unfortunately seemed to mean that he could avoid her just as effectively.

He had a suite of rooms he used as offices on the ground floor, and staff who flew in and out as if helicopters were buses. He rose at dawn and went riding every morning and never returned to the ranch for breakfast. Either he was engaged in business the rest of the day or down at the equestrian centre. But every evening they dined together in the stifling formality of the dining room.

And, terrifyingly, it was as if that confrontation several days earlier had never happened—only now there was a divide the width of the Atlantic ocean between them. Raul didn't need to walk away to hold her at a distance. He could make civil conversation, express a courteous desire to know what she had done with her day, discuss Luis and generally treat her like an honoured house guest with whom, regrettably, he didn't have very much time to spend. Oh, yes, and leave her to sleep in a guest room bed without a visible ounce of regret.

So now, when Polly espied Raul chatting to a fair-haired man in front of the state-of-the-art stables, she attempted to appear slightly surprised to run into him. She wanted to behave normally, but without giving him the impression she had deliberately sought him out.

Embarrassingly sexual butterflies erupted in her tummy as she watched him lithely straighten from his elegant lounging position against the rail. As always, he looked stupendous, black hair flopping over his bronzed brow, dark, deep-set eyes narrowed, wide shoulders outlined by a black polo shirt, lean hips and long powerful thighs sheathed in skintight jodhpurs, polished boots gleaming in the sunshine.

'Fancy seeing you here' might well be interpreted as sarcasm, so she gave Raul a purposely casual smile. Her heartbeat thundered with suppressed excitement against her breastbone, ensuring that she swiftly removed her attention from him again. 'Luis and I are just out for a walk,' she announced, and then wanted to bite her tongue out because she sounded positively fatuous.

'This is Patrick Gorman, Polly.' Raul introduced the slim, fair-haired younger man already extending his hand to her. 'He runs the breeding programme for the polo ponies.'

'Delighted to meet you, Mrs Zaforteza.'

'You're English!' Polly registered with surprise and pleasure. 'And I think I recognise that accent. Newcastle?'

'Spot on!'

Polly laughed. 'I was born in Blyth, but my parents moved south when I was six.'

'That's why you don't have a hint of a Geordie accent.' Giving her an appreciative grin, Patrick bent over the stroller. 'I'm crazy about babies!' he exclaimed, squatting down to get a closer look at Luis, where he was contentedly drowsing under the parasol. 'He's incredibly little, isn't he?'

'He's actually quite big for his age,' Polly asserted proudly, thinking how wonderfully well this supposedly accidental meeting with Raul was going, because Patrick was the chatty type which naturally helped to break the ice.

'My niece is a year old, and quite a handful last time I saw her,' Patrick told her cheerfully.

'Luis doesn't do much more than eat and sleep at the minute.'

'You have a lot of fun ahead of you,' Patrick Gorman smiled. 'Since Raul has some calls to make, would you like me to show you around this operation?'

'The calls will wait. I'll do the guided tour,' Raul slotted in smoothly, his attention darkly fixed to his animated and chattering companions.

Polly risked a glance at Raul. Brooding tension had hardened his lean, dark face. In receipt of a smouldering look, she flushed. 'Are you sure you can spare the time?' she pressed anxiously.

Disconcertingly, Raul dropped a casual arm round her taut shoulders. 'Why not?'

'Did I say something wrong back there?' Polly asked as he walked her away from the younger man.

'You talked more in two minutes to a complete stranger than you have talked to me in three entire days,' Raul delivered silkily. 'However, I would advise you to maintain a certain formal distance with Patrick.'

'Why?'

'Don't be misled by all that boyish charm. Patrick is a serial womaniser.'

Polly blinked. 'He seemed very nice. He was so interested in Luis.'

'It was just a light word of warning,' Raul drawled dismissively, his blunt cheekbones accentuated by a slight darkening of colour as she frowned at him in patent confusion over why he should have found it necessary to give that warning.

He changed the subject. 'Actually, I thought you would've been down to the stables long before now. Country-bred Englishwomen are always mad about horses. They even take their ponies to boarding school with them!' He laughed with husky appreciation. 'I expect you ride pretty well yourself.'

Conscious of the approving satisfaction he didn't attempt to conceal in his assumption that she was used to being around horses, Polly muttered, 'Er...well—'

'I've never met an Englishwoman who didn't,' Raul confided, making her tense even more. 'And, as horses are a major part of my life, that's one interest we can share.'

'I'm probably a bit rusty...riding,' Polly heard herself say, when she had *never* been on a horse in her entire life. But any wish Raul might express to share anything other than a bed deserved the maximum encouragement.

A split second later, she realised that she had just told a very stupid lie which would be easily exposed, but she had been so delighted at his talk of wanting to share his love of horses with her that she hadn't been able to bring herself to disappoint him. She would teach herself to ride, just enough to pass herself. It couldn't be that difficult, could it? In the meantime, all she had to do was make excuses.

He showed her round the stables. She copied every move he made with the horses poking their heads out over the doors. Mirroring worked a treat. Just about everything he told her went right over her head, because her knowledge of horseflesh began and ended with a childhood love of reading *Black Beauty*.

'It's all so fascinating,' she commented with a mesmerised smile while he talked about polo—an incomprehensible commentary on chukkas, throw-ins and ride-offs. His lean brown hands sketched vivid impressions to stress the fast and furious action. It occurred to her that even if he had been talking in Spanish she would still have been utterly hooked. His sheer enthusiasm had a hypnotic effect on her.

Registering the glow in her dark blue eyes as she listened to him, Raul smiled. 'You look happier today, *querida*.'

The silence that fell as he uttered the endearment seemed to thump in time with Polly's hopelessly impressionable heart. The tip of her tongue snaked out to dampen her dry lower lip. His stunning dark golden eyes homed in on the tiny movement and her tummy simply flipped. In the hot, still air, a storm of such powerful desire engulfed Polly that she quivered with embarrassment.

A slow smile curved Raul's beautiful mouth. Striding forward with confidence, he reached for her, a sudden burning brilliance blazing in his gorgeous eyes. 'You're trembling...'

And he knew why. He radiated an answering sexual heat that overwhelmed her every attempt to conceal her own reactions. And when he hauled her close with hungry hands, and plunged his mouth down passionately hard on hers, she felt as if the top of her head was flying off with excitement, and she simply went limp, eyes sliding shut, struggling to breathe, heart pounding like a manic triphammer.

'Oh, boy...' she gasped, as Raul lifted his imperious dark head again, pressing her shaken face against his shoulder. Feverishly she drank in his hot, clean scent, torn by a devouring need for him that was shatteringly intense.

But it was balanced by an awareness of *his* hunger, the jerky little shudder racking him as he snatched in a fractured breath. The barriers had come down, she sensed. He was touching her again. She was no longer off limits, like an ornament sheltering under a glass bell jar. And he wanted her, oh, yes, he wanted her, and this time that was going to be enough, she told herself urgently.

As he set her back from him, brilliant eyes veiled, Raul murmured lazily, 'I'll pick you up for a picnic lunch around three. Leave Luis at home.'

A little fretful squalling cry erupted like a comical complaint from the stroller. Raul burst out laughing. Surveying his wakening son's cross little face with a luminous pride he could not conceal, he sighed, 'We made a wonderful son together...I just wish we had made him between the sheets.'

Polly blushed, but she was touched that he should think along the same lines as she had done. 'Not much we can do about that.'

'But we'll do it the normal way the next time,' Raul asserted with amusement, and before she could even blossom at that reassuring implication that they would have another child some day, he added with deflating practicality, 'One of the grooms will run you back to the ranch. You shouldn't be out in this heat without a hat. Sunstroke is not a very pleasant experience.'

When she walked into her bedroom, two of the maids were hanging a rail of unfamiliar new garments in the wardrobe. Polly hovered, fingering rich fabrics, recognising wildly expensive designer tailoring. Dear heaven, Raul had bought her clothes. No asking, What do you like? No suggestion that she go and choose for herself. She eased a sleek dress in a smoky shade of blue from a padded hanger and held it against herself. Lordy, she'd never worn anything that short in her life!

But she was smiling, because she was already walking on air. *Next time.* Two little words that told her that Raul regarded their marriage as a lasting development. She put on the blue dress and then tracked down the housekeeper and asked for the keys of the curious little turreted building on the south boundary of the gardens. She had a couple of hours to kill, and yesterday had peered in through the shrouded windows and found the doors securely locked.

'No one goes there now, *señora*.' The older woman muttered something anxious in Spanish about *el patrón*, her kindly face strained as she finally passed over the keys with marked reluctance.

The staff might be superstitious about the place, but Polly was unconcerned by that troubled reference to *'el patrón'*. Raul wouldn't give two hoots if she went and explored. This was supposed to be her home now, and that picturesque building intrigued her.

She opened the Gothic front door and walked into a split-level, surprisingly spacious room with dust-covered furniture. The walls were faded and stained, the curtains in an advanced state of disintegration. She wandered through silent rooms, coming on a dated kitchen layered with dust before she walked up the cast-iron staircase.

There was a large bedroom, a bathroom, and then one other bedroom. She stopped in the doorway of the third room. It was a child's room, with little rusty cars still sitting on shelves, yellowing photos curling up on a noticeboard, as if the little boy had just gone away and never come back. It was eerie.

She peered at the photos. One she recognised as Raul's father. There were two portraits at the ranch that she had assumed were of Raul's parents. Eduardo, who bore a marked resemblance to Raul, and Yolanda, a regal blue-eyed blonde, who resembled him not at all. She didn't recognise the laughing brunette with the exotic tigerish eyes, although those eyes reminded her of…Raul's eyes?

The sounds of steps on the metal stairs sent Polly hurrying back out onto the landing. It was Raul, still dressed in his riding gear, breathing shallowly as if he had been hurrying.

'What are you doing poking around in here?' he demanded rawly, a savage glitter in his golden eyes, harsh lines of strain bracketing his sensual mouth.

Polly was thoroughly disconcerted by his reaction. 'I wasn't "poking around"...I was just curious. Who lived here? I didn't realise anyone had actually lived here until I came inside.'

Raul studied her fiercely and then finally lifted a wide shoulder in a jerky shrug of grudging acceptance. 'I thought you knew. Everyone knows... My family background has been exhaustively dug up and raked over by the media.'

A sense of foreboding touched Polly then, her stomach muscles clenching tight. Raul was reacting like someone in shock, his eyes flickering uneasily over their surroundings and then skimming away again, a far-away look of grim vulnerability in his eyes until he shielded them, his facial bones ferociously prominent beneath his bronzed skin.

'I lived here with my mother until I was nine,' Raul told her flatly.

'Your parents separated?' she asked in bewilderment.

Raul vented a hollow laugh. 'My mother was my father's mistress, Polly, *not* his wife!'

Floundering in shock, Polly stammered, 'B-but the blonde woman in the picture in the hall—?'

'My father's wife, Yolanda. Our lifestyle was somewhat dysfunctional.'

With a mistress in a flamboyant little house at the foot of the garden? He wasn't joking.

Raul explained in a very few words. His mother, Pilar, had been the daughter of a *llanero*, who'd worked on a neighbouring tenant's ranch. Pilar had already been pregnant with Raul when Eduardo Zaforteza married his beautiful oil heiress bride.

'When Yolanda found out about my mother, she locked the bedroom door, and my father used that as his excuse to bring us here to live,' Raul shared tautly. 'After my mother's death, he gave Yolanda half of everything he possessed to agree to my adoption.'

'What age were you when your mother died?' Polly muttered.

'Nine. There used to be a swimming pool out there. She drowned in it when she was drunk. She was frequently drunk,' Raul admitted flatly. 'What my father called "love" destroyed her...in fact it destroyed all our lives.'

'Yolanda never had any children?'

'Frequent miscarriages...*sí*, the bedroom door was unlocked eventually.' Raul grimaced. 'I think my father enjoyed having two women fighting over him. When it became a hassle, he just took off and left them to it for a while. He and Yolanda died in a plane crash almost ten years ago.'

Nausea was stirring in Polly's sensitive stomach. All of a sudden she was seeing and understanding so much, but recoiling from a vision of the distressing scenes which Raul must have witnessed as he grew up. An unhappy mother with a drink problem. No normal family life, no secure childhood, nothing but tangled adult relationships and constant strife.

She was imagining how much the wronged wife must have loathed Raul and his mother, and didn't even want to consider what it had been like for Raul to live in the same house with Yolanda from the tender age of nine. An embittered woman, who had forced her husband to pay for the right to adopt his illegitimate son. Little wonder Raul found it a challenge to believe in love or the deeper bonds of marriage.

'You should have this place cleared out.' Polly strove for a brisk tone.

'I haven't set foot here in years. It was my father who insisted it stay as it was. He liked to come here when he felt sentimental,' Raul said with lethal derision.

Polly was frankly appalled by what he had told her, but working hard to hide it. She was annoyed that she had blundered in to rouse such unpleasant memories, and exasperated that she hadn't had more interest that long-ago day at the library in learning about Raul's background rather than about the women in his life. She started down the curving staircase, eager to be out in the fresh air again.

'I'll have this place emptied, then...OK?' Polly pressed, seeking agreement for what she saw as a necessary act.

Raul shrugged with comforting unconcern. The distant look had gone from his eyes as he scrutinised her appearance and his mouth quirked. 'So the clothes have arrived...I chose them when I was in Caracas. At least you've got something decent to wear until you do your own shopping,' he pointed out, for all the world as if she had been walking around in rags.

Half an hour later, they got into a four-wheel drive to head out for the picnic he had promised. They left the asphalt lanes that criss-crossed the vast spread of the ranch buildings to hurtle down a dusty trail and then out across the grassy plains. All sign of modern civilisation was left behind within minutes. Yellow poplars, gum trees and the ubiquitous palm grew in thickets on higher ground, where the floodwater hadn't reached. Great flocks of exotic multi-coloured birds rose from the trees with shrill cries as they passed.

The sky was a clear, cloudless turquoise over the sun-drenched savannah. It was a strange and unfamiliar terrain to Polly, yet the *llanos*, teaming with wildlife in their isolation, had a haunting, fascinating beauty.

'Where are we going?' she finally asked.

'Wait and see,' Raul advised lazily.

He brought the car to a halt and sprang out. As she followed, all she could see was a dense line of trees. Raul pulled a hamper out of the back seat. They walked under the trees, and then she caught her breath. In a gently sloping hidden valley below them, a waterfall tumbled down over ancient weathered rocks into a reed-edged lagoon.

'Once a tributary of the Orinoco river ran through here...this is all that remains.' Raul set the hamper down on the lush grass in the shade of the coconut palms.

Polly was enchanted. 'It's so peaceful.'

'My mother brought me here as a child. This place was special to her,' Raul confided. 'I suspect I might have been conceived here.'

'Don't you have any family left alive?' Polly asked as she sat down.

Raul swung round to look at her, his fabulous bone structure tensing, dark eyes sombre in the sunlight. 'My grandfather, Fidelio.' Raul shrugged. 'He disowned my mother. He's a very proud old man, and still refuses to acknowledge our relationship, but I told him about Luis last week.'

'I'm sorry I've been so prickly and awkward,' Polly said abruptly.

Raul gave her a slanting smile as he sank down beside her. 'I've been awkward too. This...you and I...it's all new to me.'

That rueful smile touched something deep inside her. Rising up on her knees, Polly took her courage in both hands. Planting her palms against his chest, she pushed him flat.

Startled, Raul gazed up at her, and then a wolfish grin slashed his face. 'And I was going to be a gentleman, *gatita*. I was planning to wait until you'd eaten! But, since we are both of one mind...' Raul murmured, taking pity on her as she hovered above him, uncertain of what to do next, and reaching up to slowly draw her down to him.

He sent his hands skimming down to her slim hips and eased her into the cradle of his long, muscular thighs with an erotic suggestiveness that was as bold as it was unashamed. Melded to every virile line of his powerful body, Polly turned boneless. He undid the zip on her dress and tipped it down off her shoulders.

Her firm breasts rose and fell inside the delicate cups of her lace bra. He unclipped the bra and curved appreciative hands over the pale, pouting curves that tumbled out. She gave a muffled gasp as he tugged at her straining nipples and arched her back, excitement seizing her in its hold.

Raul flipped her over gently onto her back. Vaulting upright, he proceeded to remove his clothes with a lack of cool that only excited her more. She lifted her hips, tugged down the dress, sat up to shyly dispose of her remaining garments—but all the time she was covertly watching him. As that superb bronze body emerged she was enthralled, mouth bone-dry, pulses accelerating.

A delicious little quiver of anticipation made her ache. Just looking at him, seeing the potent evidence of his desire for her, stole her breath away. He was so aroused she could feel herself melting into a liquid pool of submission. And when he returned to her she was already on fire, the swollen pink buds of her breasts begging for his attention, a sensation of damp heat throbbing almost painfully between her thighs.

His stunning eyes read the message in hers. He came down to her and kissed her breathless with a force of hunger that overwhelmed her own. 'I feel wild...' he groaned with a ragged laugh. 'One more night watching you across the dining table and I would've pulled you under it!'

'It didn't show.'

'*Infierno*...I get as hard as a rock just being in the same room with you,' Raul growled rawly. 'I don't think I have ever been so frustrated in my life! I was tempted to take you into the stables earlier and...' As her dark blue eyes widened in open shock at that series of blunt revelations, he compressed his lips, a dark rise of blood emphasising his cheekbones. 'I just want you so much I can't think of anything else right now.'

Polly was dazed by that almost apologetic conclusion. She had never once dreamt that Raul might come to desire her to such an extent. Colliding with devouring golden eyes, she shivered. He meshed a not quite steady hand into her hair.

'That's all right,' she mumbled, mesmerised by his intensity but even weaker now with wanton longing. 'I want you too.'

Heat flooded her as he kneed her legs apart. He had said

he felt wild, and what he did to her *was* wild. Nothing could have prepared her for the storm of powerful need he released. He took her hard and fast, and then so slowly and so agonisingly sweetly that she was plunged into a mindless glory of acute pleasure, afterwards savouring every precious moment of satiated contentment in his arms, certain that they had turned a corner to forge deeper bonds.

She slept for a while then. She wakened, feeling ridiculously shy, to focus on Raul, where he lay fully dressed again in a careless sprawl, an unusually peaceful aspect to his stillness. Assuming he was asleep, she sat up. His lashes were as lush as black silk fans, his sensual mouth relaxed in repose, dark stubble already outlining his stubborn jawline. She could not resist running a loving finger down gently over one proud cheekbone.

He opened his eyes and she froze, like a thief caught in the act.

Whipping up a hand, he closed his fingers round her wrist and planted a kiss to the damp centre of her palm. 'You make me feel good,' he confided softly.

And the rush of love that surged through her in response left her dizzy.

Raul sat up, still retaining a light hold on her hand, and dealt her a wry look. 'How do you feel about having another baby in about nine months?'

'I…I b-beg your pardon?'

'I didn't take any precautions…' Raul raised two expressive hands, clearly primed for a furious outburst. 'I just didn't think…I was very excited.'

Hugging the dress he must have tossed over her while she slept, Polly reflected that he had gone from never having taken that risk to repeating it over and over again with a devastating lack of inhibition. But then she was his wife—once a chosen baby machine, she conceded rather sourly. No doubt he imagined it would be no big deal for her to find herself pregnant again so soon. But right at that moment Polly cringed at the prospect of her freshly slender and now apparently sexually attractive shape vanishing again. Raul wouldn't find her remotely attractive any more and he might stray, she thought fearfully.

'I'm sorry...' Raul breathed tightly as the silence stretched and stretched.

'It's all right for you...you're not going to get all fat and clumsy, are you?'

Instantly Raul closed an arm round her. 'You were not fat and clumsy...you were gorgeous.'

'You like babies. You're not likely to tell me the truth—and I've never been gorgeous in my life!' Polly added for good measure.

'Why did I find you so tempting while you were in the clinic, then?'

Polly stilled. 'Did you?'

'I thought you were incredibly sexy...like a lush, ripe peach.'

She supposed peaches were at least round. But she looked at him, saw his sincerity and swallowed hard on another tart retort. 'My body hasn't settled down yet,' she shared, striving not to be prim about discussing such a thing with him. 'So I don't know how much of a risk there is.'

As Polly shimmied back into her dress, Raul glanced at his watch and swore succinctly in Spanish. 'Caramba...look at the time—and we have guests coming to dinner!'

As she stood up, Raul zipped her dress for her. She was conscious of her body's decided tenderness, the result of their frantic lovemaking. He was oversexed, as well as careless, but she still loved him to death. Otherwise she probably would have killed him at that moment for simply dropping on her this late in the day the fact that they were entertaining guests.

'Who's coming?' she asked, balancing to slide into her second shoe.

'Melina D'Agnolo and—' A firm hand snaked out swiftly to steady her as she staggered on one leg and nearly went headlong down the slope. '*Dios mío, mi esposa*…take care!' Raul urged.

'You were saying?' Her head bent to conceal her shock, Polly breathed in very shakily.

'Melina, our closest neighbour,' Raul shared, with what Polly considered to be megawatt cool. 'She grew up on the ranch she's currently renting from the estate. She's bringing the Drydons—mutual friends. Patrick will join us. He used to work for Rob Drydon.'

'I'll enjoy meeting them.' Polly sneaked a glance at Raul to see if he looked even slightly self-conscious. He didn't.

Raul swept up the hamper and even joked about the fact that they had eaten nothing. They strolled back to the car. Raul helped her into the passenger seat.

'I'm a brute,' he murmured, scanning the bluish shadows of tiredness under her eyes. 'But it was fantastic, *es verdad*!'

Melina was a neighbour. The *llanos* looked empty for miles and miles, but they harboured the poisonous Melina somewhere close by. It was ghastly news. Worse, Raul expected her to entertain his ex-mistress. He was cooler than an ice cube. But then he wasn't aware that she knew about that former relationship. *Former*, she emphasised to herself with determination.

Raul was a sophisticated male and she was being naive. His intimate relationship with Melina D'Agnolo might be over, but that didn't mean he would cut her out of his life altogether. She had to taken an adult view of this social encounter.

# CHAPTER TEN

'I AM so very pleased for you both,' Melina murmured, with a look of deep sincerity in her green eyes as she reached for Polly's hand in an open and friendly manner.

Dear heaven, she could act me off the stage, Polly registered in dismay, not having been prepared for quite so impressive a pretence. Stunning, in a black lace dress which clung to her superb figure like a second skin, Melina curved a light hand over Raul's sleeve and recounted a witty little story which made him laugh.

Polly had been feeling really good in her scarlet off-the-shoulder dress—until just before she came downstairs. Now her head was aching. She hoped Melina's pleasantries were more than surface-deep.

Rob Drydon and his wife, Susie, were from Texas, and eagerly talking horses with Patrick Gorman. As they transferred to the dining room Melina was in full flow of conversation with Raul, and Polly was left to trail behind them. Patrick caught up with her.

'The *condesa* will walk all over you if you let her,' he whispered in her ear.

Polly's eyes widened. She glanced up at him.

Patrick gave her a rueful look. 'The scene she threw on your arrival was too good a story for the staff to keep quiet. I heard the grooms talking about it,' he confided. 'And as Raul needs the least protection of any male I know, why is he the only person around here who *doesn't* know about the warm welcome you received?'

Polly tensed. 'There wasn't any need to involve him.'

'If you'd involved Raul, she wouldn't be here now, spoiling your evening,' Patrick dropped gently.

As Patrick tucked Polly into her chair at the foot of the table she encountered Raul's level scrutiny, and found herself flushing without knowing why. Picking up her wine glass, she drank.

'Raul told me to pick out a decent mount for you,' Patrick shared chattily.

Polly's wine went down the wrong way. She spluttered, cleared her throat, and gave her companion a pleading look. 'Can you keep a secret, Patrick?'

He nodded.

Leaning her head guiltily close to his, Polly whispered, 'I'm afraid I wasn't entirely honest about my riding ability.'

Patrick frowned. 'In what way?'

'I've never been on a horse in my life.'

After a startled pause, Patrick burst out laughing.

'Don't be selfish,' Raul drawled silkily. 'Share the joke with the rest of us.'

Clashing with shimmering dark eyes, Polly flushed. 'It wasn't really funny enough.'

'The English sense of humour isn't the same as ours,' Melina remarked sweetly. 'I've always found it rather juvenile.'

Patrick grinned. 'I have to confess I'm not into your wildly dramatic soap operas. Each to his own.'

Under cover of the ensuing conversation, Patrick murmured, 'See you tomorrow morning at six while Raul's out riding. I'll teach you enough to pass yourself, and then you can tell him you're just not very good and he can take over.'

'You're a saviour,' Polly muttered with real gratitude, and turned to address Rob Drydon.

After dinner, they settled down with drinks in the drawing room. Melina crossed the room with another one of her super-friendly smiles, saying in her clear, ringing voice, 'I want you to tell me all about yourself, Polly.'

Sinking deep into the sofa, to show the maximum possible amount of her incredibly long and shapely legs, Melina asked, 'So how's married life treating you?'

'Wonderfully well.' Polly emptied her glass in one gulp and prayed for deliverance, uneasily conscious that Raul was watching them both from the other side of the room. She wished she was feeling more herself.

'I don't think Raul likes to see you drinking so much. He rarely touches alcohol...the occasional glass of champagne on important occasions.' Registering Polly's surprise, Melina elevated a brow. 'So you didn't know? How couldn't you know something that basic about your own husband?'

Polly clutched her empty glass like a drunkard amongst teetotallers, bitterly, painfully resenting the fact that Melina could tell her anything she didn't know about Raul. It reminded her all over again that until very recently there had been nothing normal about her relationship with Raul.

'That's none of your business,' she told Melina flatly, determined not to play the blonde's spiteful double game. Now, when it was too late, she saw how foolish she had been not to tell Raul about her initial clash with Melina. If she tried to tell him now, he probably wouldn't believe her, not with Melina putting on the show of the century with her smiling friendliness.

'Raul *is* my business, and he always will be,' Melina said smugly. 'Did you make a huge scene when he came to see me that very same night?'

Polly froze and then slowly, jerkily turned her head, which was beginning to pound unpleasantly. 'What are you saying?'

'That even I wasn't expecting him quite *that* soon.' Glinting green eyes absorbed Polly's growing pallor with satisfaction. 'I didn't need ESP to realise that you'd obviously had a colossal row. It was your first night in your new home and yet Raul ended up with me.'

'You're lying...I don't believe you.' That night had been the equivalent of their wedding night. Raul couldn't have—

he simply couldn't have gone to Melina beforehand! But he *had* gone out riding. In sick desperation, she strained to recall what he had told her. Hadn't he admitted calling in with a neighbour? Numbly, Polly let the maid refill her glass. Melina was a neighbour. Technically Raul hadn't lied to her...

'He came to me to talk. Raul needs a woman, not a little girl.'

Polly took a defiant slug of her drink. 'He needs you like he needs a hole in the head!' she said, and then frowned in confusion as Melina suddenly leant past her to start talking in low-pitched Spanish.

'I hope you're feeling better the next time I see you, Polly,' Melina then murmured graciously as she rose to her feet.

An icy voice like a lethal weapon breathed in Polly's shrinking ear, 'I'll see our guests out, *mi esposa*. Don't you dare get up. If you stand up, you might fall over, and if you fall over, I'll put you under a very cold shower!'

Devastated to realise that Raul must have overheard her last response to Melina, and doubtless believed that she had been inexcusably rude for no good reason, Polly sat transfixed while everyone took their leave, loads of sympathetic looks and concerned murmurs coming her way once Raul mentioned that she was feeling dizzy.

Patrick hung back to say with a frown, 'Do you think you'll make it down to the stables in the morning?'

Polly nodded with determination.

Recalling how wonderfully close she and Raul had been earlier in the day, Polly began to droop. *Had* Raul been with Melina that night? Only a fool would believe anything Melina said, she decided. But a split second later she was thinking the worst again, imagining how easy, how tempting it would have been for Raul in the mood he had been in to seek consolation with his mistress, a beautiful, self-assured woman whom he had known for so many years...

Two minutes later, Raul strode back in and scooped Polly off the sofa.

'I'm so miserable!' Polly suddenly sobbed in despair.

Taken aback, Raul tightened his arms around her and murmured what sounded like soothing things in Spanish.

'And I haven't had too much to drink…I just feel *awful*!' she wept, clutching at the lapel of his dinner jacket and then freeing him again, because she didn't want to touch him, didn't want to be close to him in any way if he was capable of such deception.

Raul carried her upstairs, laid her gently down on his bed and slipped off her shoes.

'I'm in agony with a headache!' Polly suddenly hurled.

'You're tipsy,' Raul murmured with total conviction as he unzipped her dress.

'My head's so sore,' Polly mumbled, drowning in self-pity.

Raul extracted her from her dress and deftly massaged her taut shoulders. 'You're so tense,' he scolded. 'Relax, I'll get some painkillers.'

Hadn't he heard what she had said to Melina after all? Had she jumped to conclusions? Surely he would have said something by now?

'Why were you angry with me?' she whispered.

'You were flirting like mad with Patrick.'

'I like him,' Polly muttered, distracted by that unexpected response.

'I *know*,' Raul growled, in an undertone that set up a chain reaction down her sensitive spine as he undid her bra and deftly disposed of it. 'I didn't realise you were feeling ill. I was surprised you were drinking so much.'

'I knew I had a bad head when I came downstairs,' Polly sighed, wriggling her way out of her tights at his behest. 'I felt rotten.'

'You should've told me,' Raul purred. 'Melina said you were talking about our annual fiesta here…were you?'

Polly tensed. 'Don't remember…my head was splitting. You seem to know her very well.'

'Inside out,' Raul agreed silkily.

'When did you invite Melina to dinner?'

'The same evening I visited my grandfather. Fidelio is the foreman of the ranch Melina rents,' Raul revealed.

'Oh… Oh…' Polly gasped slightly, slowly putting that together for herself.

Raul had called in with Fidelio that night to tell him he had a great-grandson. And that was why Raul had seen Melina. How silly she had been! And why hadn't it occurred to her before now that at some point Raul would have *had* to see Melina face to face to inform her of his marriage? As she came to terms with that rational explanation, a giant tide of relief started rolling over her.

'I'm awfully tired,' she confessed.

Raul tugged her up against him and gently slotted her into the silky pyjama jacket he had fetched. He carefully rolled up the sleeves. 'I have a villa on the coast. I think we should spend a few days there…'

'Sounds good,' Polly mumbled, and closed her eyes.

She slept like a log but she had the most terrifying dream. She was living in the house at the foot of the garden and Melina was queening it at the ranch. History repeating itself in reverse. She woke with a start, perspiring and shivering, just in time to see Raul reach the door in his riding gear.

'What time is it?'

'Only five-thirty…go back to sleep.'

Abruptly recalling the arrangement she had made with Patrick Gorman, Polly leapt out of bed the instant Raul closed the door behind him.

After a quick shower, she pulled on jeans and a T-shirt, frantic because she knew she was running late. She rushed down the corridor to see Luis, which was always the first thing she did in the morning. In the doorway of the nursery, she stopped dead in surprise and some dismay.

Raul was lounging back in a chair with Luis lying asleep on top of him. Garbed in a little yellow sleepsuit and sprawled trustingly across his father's muscular chest, their son looked impossibly small in comparison.

'I thought you'd already left...' Her voice drained away again, because all of a sudden she felt the weight of her silly deception. It hit her the instant she registered what going behind Raul's back actually entailed.

Brilliant dark eyes veiled, Raul gave her a glinting smile that had the odd effect of increasing her discomfiture. 'If you feed him, Luis is very appealing at this hour.'

'You fed him yourself?' Polly was astonished.

'Since I woke him up by coming in, it didn't seem fair not to. He went through that bottle like he hadn't eaten in days!' Raul confided, smoothing light fingers down over his son's back as Luis snuffled and shifted his little froglike legs, content as only a baby with a full tummy can be. 'His nursemaid changed him for me. He looks so fragile stripped, I didn't want to run the risk of doing it myself.'

Polly reached down and stole Luis into her own arms, and lovingly rubbed her cheek against her son's soft, sweet-smelling skin before she reluctantly tucked him back into his cot.

'I gather the jeans mean you've finally decided to come out riding with me,' Raul drawled from the door. 'You won't find those jeans very comfortable...but then I assume you already know that.'

Still leaning over the cot with her back turned to him, Polly's jaw dropped.

'You're lucky I stopped off in here. You'd have missed me otherwise,' Raul added casually.

Outside the silent house, Polly clambered into the four-wheel drive with a trapped look in her eyes.

'It's been ages and ages since I've been on a horse, Raul,' she said, rather abruptly.

'It's a skill you never forget,' Raul asserted bracingly.

'A couple of hours in the saddle and you'll wonder how you ever lived without it.'

A couple of *hours*? Polly was aghast. Raul shot the vehicle to a halt at the side of the stables.

Patrick Gorman strolled out of the big tack room and then froze when he saw Raul.

'I'm not accustomed to seeing you abroad at this hour, Patrick. Polly's coming out with me this morning.'

'I'll be in the office if you want me.' Without even risking a glance in Polly's direction, Patrick strode off.

Polly stood like a graven image while a pair of grooms led out two mounts. El Lobo, Raul's big black stallion, and a doe-eyed bay mare—who looked, somewhat reassuringly, barely awake.

Raul planted a hard hat on her head and did up the strap. Then he extended a peculiarly shaped garment that reminded her of an oversized body warmer.

'Protection...since you mentioned being out of practice. If you take a toss, I don't want you hurt.' He fed her into the ugly bulky protector and deftly pushed home the clasps. It weighed her down like armour.

Sweeping her up, Raul settled her into the saddle, where she hunched in sudden complete terror.

'I can't ride... Raul, do you hear me? I can't ride!' Polly cried.

'I know...' Raul murmured, so softly she had to strain to hear him as he shortened the stirrups and slotted her feet into them. 'I'd have to be a complete idiot not to know.'

'You *kn-know*?' Polly gasped in disbelief as he swung up on El Lobo with fluid ease.

'*Dios mío*...how could I not guess? Your body language around the horses yesterday was not that of an experienced horsewoman. And I could hardly miss the fact that you hadn't a clue what I was talking about,' Raul delineated very drily.

Polly turned a dull red. 'I thought you'd find it a complete bore if I admitted I was a greenhorn.'

His stunning dark golden eyes gleamed with grim amusement. 'Are you really so naive about men? Is there any male who doesn't relish imparting his superior knowledge of a subject to a woman?'

'I told Patrick I couldn't ride last night…he offered to take me through the basics this morning,' she volunteered in an embarrassed rush. 'It was stupid of me.'

In response, Raul shot her a chilling glance as piercing as an arrow of ice. His lean, strong face was hard. '*Infierno!* I suspected something of the sort last night. Let me tell you now that I do not expect my wife to make furtive assignations with my employees!'

'It *wasn't* an assign—'

'And from now on you will ensure that you are never in Patrick Gorman's company without the presence of a third party.'

Thoroughly taken aback, Polly exclaimed, 'Don't be ridiculous!'

His brilliant eyes flashed. 'As your husband, I have the right to demand a certain standard of behaviour from you.'

Polly was outraged and mortified. 'But you're being totally unreasonable. ''The presence of a third party''!' she repeated in a fuming undertone of incredulity.

'If you disobey me, I'll dismiss him.'

Raul held her shaken eyes with fierce intensity, and then simply switched channels by telling her that she was sitting on the mare's back like a seasick sack of potatoes. The riding lesson which followed stretched Polly's self-discipline to the limits. She had to rise above that abrasive exchange and concentrate on his instructions, and Raul had high expectations.

Finally, Raul led her out onto the *llanos* at a walking pace. 'You're doing very well for a greenhorn, *mi esposa*,' he drawled, surprising her.

Polly focused on his darkly handsome features. As her tummy lurched with reaction, she despised herself. Not an hour ago Raul had been talking like a Middle Eastern potentate who thought no woman could be trusted alone with a man.

A frown line forming between his brows, Raul reined in his mount a few minutes later. A rider was approaching them—an elderly *llanero* with a bristling silver moustache, clad in an old-fashioned poncho and a wide-brimmed hat.

Raul addressed him in Spanish.

'My grandfather, Fidelio Navarro,' he told Polly flatly.

With a sober look of acknowledgement, his posture in the saddle rigid, the older man responded in softly spoken Spanish. He was as unyielding as Raul. Polly glanced between them in frustration. Raul and his grandfather greeted each other like strangers, each as scrupulously formal and rigid with unbending pride as the other.

Polly leant out of the saddle to extend her hand, a warm and determined smile on her face. After some hesitation, Fidelio Navarro moved his mount closer and briefly clasped her hand. 'It would please me very much if you came to see our son, Luis,' Polly said quietly.

'He doesn't speak English,' Raul breathed icily.

Not daring to look at him, conscious that he was angrily disconcerted by her intervention, Polly tilted her chin. 'Then please translate my invitation. And could you also tell him that as I have neither parents nor grandparents living, it would mean a great deal to me if Luis was given the chance to know his great-grandfather?'

Silence followed, a silence screaming with tension and Raul's outright incredulity.

Then Raul spoke at some length. His grandfather met Polly's hopeful gaze and sombrely replied.

'He thanks you for your warmth and generosity,' Raul interpreted woodenly. 'He will think the idea over.'

But there had been more than that in Fidelio's sun-creased dark eyes: a slight defrosting of his discomfiture, an easing of the rigidity round his unsmiling mouth. As they parted to ride off in different directions, she heard Raul release his breath in a stark hiss.

'*Caramba!* How can you justify such interference in what is nothing to do with you?' Raul gritted in a tone of raw disbelief that actually shook with the strength of his emotion. 'Do you think I have not already invited him to my home without success?'

'Well, if you glower at him like that when you ask, I'm not surprised. Maybe he thought you were only asking out of politeness, privately recognising the relationship without really wanting to get any closer...' Daringly, Polly proffered her own suspicions. 'I think you and Fidelio are both so scared of losing face that you're afraid to talk frankly to each other.'

'I am afraid of nothing, and how you can *dare*—'

'I did it for Luis,' Polly lied, because she had spoken up first and foremost for Raul's benefit—Raul, who definitely wanted closer ties with his grandfather. 'Neither of us have any other family to offer him.'

'What do *I* know about family?' Raul growled, spurring on El Lobo in the direction of the ranch.

'What do I know either?' Polly thought of her own less than perfect childhood, with her controlling, judgemental father. 'But we *are* a family now, and we can learn like everybody else!'

'A family?' Raul repeated in frowning acknowledgement, and with perceptible disconcertion. 'I suppose we are.'

Only sparing the time to inform her that they were leaving for his villa on the Caribbean coast that afternoon, Raul took his leave. Polly went for a bath to ease her tired muscles. It was all swings and roundabouts with Raul, she thought heavily. One moment he was alienating her with his tyrannical and utterly unreasonable threat to dismiss Patrick Gorman simply because *she* had unthinkingly stepped over the formal boundary lines Raul expected her to maintain. And the next?

The next, Raul was filling her with an almost overwhelming desire to close her arms round him in comfort

and reassurance. For Raul, she recognised, the years between birth and adulthood had been dogged by traumatic
experiences.

What had it been like for him? The son of Eduardo
Zaforteza's mistress, his mother isolated by a relationship
that had been flaunted rather than more acceptably concealed. Behind her lover's back, Pilar must have been
shunned and despised, and how had that affected Raul?
Until his father had adopted him, nothing had been certain
or safe in Raul's life.

Raul must have developed his own defences at an early
age. After his mother's death, he'd lived as a bitter bone
of contention in a destructive, acrimonious marriage. He
had once remarked that in disputes between couples the
child was often the weapon, that she had to know that as
well as *he* did, only at the time she hadn't picked up on
what he was telling her about his own background. In the
same way, she remembered his unexpected outrage when
she had made a crack about what he might consider a 'decent mother'. She had never dreamt what a sensitive subject
that might be, and now winced at the recollection.

Finally she was beginning to understand the man she
loved, but her dismay increased in proportion to that new
understanding. At some stage in that damaged childhood
and adolescence Raul had begun protecting himself, by
keeping emotional ties that might threaten his equanimity
on a superficial level. It showed in his relationships with
women, even in his hopelessly defensive attitude to his es-
tranged grandfather. He didn't risk himself, he held back,
and yet he didn't hold back with Luis, Polly conceded painfully. He loved their son with unashamed intensity, and was
content, indeed happy to focus his emotions on their child.

And that meant that she herself was still chasing hopes
that were unattainable. Raul would never love her. If their
marriage was to survive, she had to get her priorities in
order and stop expecting more from Raul than he was ca-

pable of giving her. And yet, according to Melina, a little
voice gibed with cruel effect, he had *loved* her…

Sprawled with elegant indolence on the rattan seating, a
look of amusement on his bronzed features, Raul studied
Polly while she watched the dancers on the beach with
unconcealed fascination. The *tambores*—African drums
made out of hollow logs—supplied the frenzied beat for the
male and female figures twisting and shaking with aban-
donment.

'I thought you would enjoy this,' Raul murmured with
lazy satisfaction. 'That's why I organised it.'

Meeting his stunning dark golden eyes, Polly burned.
She had to drag her attention back to the dancers. The intensely sensual movements of the gyrating couples were
becoming ever wilder.

Raul curved a long arm round her and she felt her whole
body quicken with instant awareness. Over the past twelve
days Raul had taught her to value every hour that they spent
together, and every morning she got up, apprehensively
waiting for him to announce that they were leaving the
villa. After all, this coming weekend the fiesta would be
held at the ranch. But right now Polly wanted time to stand
still, because here nothing else seemed to touch them.

Raul made a lot of phone calls and used a computer to
stay in touch with the world of business, but he was with
her almost all the time, more relaxed and less restless and
driven than she had ever known him to be. He never
seemed bored. In fact he was rather like he had been in
Vermont, she registered, with slight surprise at that acknowledgement. Talking to her, interested in her, amusing,
entertaining, even tender, all the tension gone, the sole difference being that sexual intimacy now deepened their relationship.

As the dance appeared to be reaching a climax, Polly
was astonished when another woman stepped in. With fran-

tically twitching hips she shoved the original female dancer away from the male and triumphantly took her place.

'A comment on the fickleness of the male sex,' Raul drawled, amused at her bemused frown over such an unromantic development. 'You're so innocent, *querida*.'

Not so innocent, Polly reflected tensely, enervated by that unexpected change of partners that came too close for comfort to her own deepest fears.

How long was she going to live with the secret terror that Raul might some day return to his discreet liaison with Melina D'Agnolo? Melina had already made it abundantly clear that she was prepared to wait for him, and no doubt she was equally ready to do whatever it might take to get him back. When would fidelity become a challenge to a male who didn't love her? At what stage would her novelty value in the marital bed become boring and predictable? Disturbed by the insecure thoughts with which she was tormenting herself, Polly shut them down.

After thanking the dancers, they went back indoors to the marbled splendour of the spacious villa. Set beside a secluded palm-fringed beach of golden sand, complete with crystal-clear water to bathe in, the villa rejoiced in the surroundings of a tropical paradise.

They tiptoed in to see Luis, out for the count in his cot. Raul curved his arms round her from behind. 'He really *is* special,' he said huskily.

'Naturally…he's yours,' Polly teased. 'And because he's your son, he is the most super-intelligent and advanced baby on this planet!'

'You think so too, *querida*,' he reminded her in a sensual growl as he slowly spun her round to crush her soft, willing mouth hungrily under his own. Her body sang with feverish hot excitement.

He carried her through to their bedroom and settled her on the bed, standing over her, intent golden eyes roaming over her slender length with the bold and unashamed desire that never failed to ease her secret fears. How could Raul want her so much and have room to even think of any other woman? How could he make love to her day after day and night after night with a seemingly insatiable appetite for her body and find anything lacking in her?

In heaven, Polly closed her eyes as he peeled off her clothes, piece by tantalising piece, pausing to kiss and caress every newly revealed curve and line of her until there wasn't a single part of her quivering, wantonly aroused being that didn't ache for him to possess her.

'I'm going to teach you to dance like that with me,' Raul murmured.

Polly's eyes opened very wide on his devastatingly handsome face. He actually looked serious.

'But only in private. I don't want anyone else seeing the way you look at me, the way you move against me...' he admitted hoarsely.

He was so intense about sex. In fact, for someone who had informed her that sex was merely another physical appetite, Raul seemed to be set on proving that every time he touched her it was another variation on an endlessly fascinating theme that pretty much absorbed him more with every passing day. He couldn't keep his hands off her. He had gone from being a male who was not remotely tactile out of bed to a male who usually had her anchored in some way to him no matter where they were.

She framed his cheekbones with possessive hands and let the tip of her tongue dart provocatively between his lips. With a groan of hunger, Raul practically flattened her to the bed and kissed her with a fierce sexual need that melted her skin over her bones. And all cool was abandoned at that point.

A long while later, she lay limp with satiation while Raul abstractedly wound a strand of her hair round a long brown forefinger. 'Tell me about the first time you fell in love,' he invited without warning.

Polly glanced at him in surprise. Raul didn't ask things like that. And it was an awkward question. One crush and one short-lived infatuation were all she had to talk about, barring himself.

He shrugged a bare bronzed shoulder. 'Curiosity.'

'He was called—'

'I don't want to know his name,' Raul intervened instantly, jawline hardening.

Somewhat disconcerted by that interruption, Polly breathed, 'Yes...er, well, he was another student—'

'I don't need to know that either...what I want to know is how you *felt*,' Raul stressed.

'How I...felt,' Polly echoed. 'Silly and dizzy, and then gutted about covers it. The minute I got to know what he was really like, I couldn't understand what I'd seen in him.'

'You fell out of love again that fast...what did he *do*?' Raul enquired darkly, raising himself up to stare down at her.

'He hustled me into a bedroom one lunchtime and told me it was my lucky day.'

She now had Raul's interest. 'You're kidding?'

'When I said no, he got abusive. He thought I'd be a push-over.'

'Major misjudgement,' Raul framed, a slight shake in his dark, deep voice. 'How old was this guy?'

'Nineteen.'

'All teenage boys think about is scoring.'

'You weren't much older when you and Melina...I mean—' Biting back the remainder of that impulsive remark, Polly coloured at the sudden narrowing of the shrewd dark eyes above hers. 'Well, she mentioned you'd once been an item.'

'Did she really?' His black spiky lashes screened his gaze, his wide, sensual mouth hardening on that information.

Polly lowered her eyes, more disturbed by that silence than she would have been by any explanation. Why was it that the unknown was always so much more threatening?

'We'll fly home on Friday morning,' Raul informed her.

'But the fiesta...' Polly groaned, torn between relief and anxiety. 'There must be loads of arrangements to make, and I haven't even made a start—'

'After all these years of practice, the staff could stage it on their own.' Rolling over onto his back, Raul reached for her again. His gleaming scrutiny raked over her pink face with unsettling efficiency. 'Have I ever told you how extraordinarily expressive those gorgeous blue eyes are, *mi esposa*?' he asked huskily. 'Do you know they close every time I kiss you?'

Polly studied him with the focused intensity of a woman in love, a kind of agony coiling tight as a spring inside her. If he betrayed her, she would die. If their marriage ended, her future would end with it. She could not bear to think of life without him. She wanted to cling like a vine, but clinging would be as much out of order as probing personal questions which might well have answers she'd be better off not hearing.

And suddenly he *was* kissing her again, evoking a wild hunger that clawed at her slim body, awakening all over again that frantic, feverish, elemental need that overwhelmed every restraint and blanked out every thought.

Polly woke up alone on the morning of their departure. There was nothing unusual about that. It was a challenge to keep Raul in bed after dawn. Early rising and a two-hour break at midday were the norm in Venezuela. Trying not to feel sad that they were leaving the villa, she went for a shower.

As she leafed through a wardrobe that had grown mightily in size since leaving the ranch, she hugged precious memories of their stay to herself. Strolling hand in hand along the Paseo Colón boulevard in Puerta la Cruz, enjoying the cool breezes coming in off the ocean; speeding in a motor launch through the eerie mangroves in the Mochina National Park; eating crispy *churros* with hot chocolate for breakfast *and* supper on Margarita Island; driving up to

Caracas to shop in the CCCT and Paseo las Mercedes malls, discovering that there *was* such a thing as a male who loved shopping and indeed that there were no greater worshippers of the consumer society or the art of being beautiful than the Venezuelans.

She was happy—yes, she had to admit it, she was very, very happy. Feeling good in a beautifully tailored leaf-green short skirt and top, she glanced into Luis's room and smiled at the sight of the empty cot. Luis was probably sitting in his infant seat watching his father work and enjoying a somewhat one-sided conversation in between times.

She could already hear Raul talking as she reached the door of the room he had been using as an office.

'…am I bored?' Raul was saying with husky amusement. 'On my honeymoon, Melina?' And then, ruefully, 'I'm *thinking* in English these days!'

Polly froze in her tracks. Her heart was thumping so hard it felt as if it was banging in her ears, and she had to strain to hear. The silence went on and on. She peered round the door lintel and glimpsed Raul, poised with his back to the door, wide shoulders bunching with tension below the superb cut of his lightweight cream jacket, bronzed fingers beating out a rapid soundless tattoo on the edge of the desk.

'Of course I appreciate your loyalty, Melina,' Raul continued in a roughened sexy undertone. 'I'm looking forward to seeing you tonight too. No, I don't think it should be too difficult. I'm not on a leash yet.'

# CHAPTER ELEVEN

'YOU still look rough. You should lie down,' Raul decreed as he walked Polly up the steps into the ranch.

'What about the fiesta…all the people coming?' Polly mumbled sickly, edging away from him as soon as she decently could.

'It's been happening for over a hundred years without you, *mi esposa*,' Raul responded in a teasing tone as he bent to lift her gently up into his arms and stride towards the magnificent staircase. 'Just go to bed and stay there until you feel better. That's the only important thing.'

Shock had unsettled her stomach. She had been sick during the flight, convincing Raul that she had caught some bug. He could not have been more caring and concerned had she developed a life-threatening illness. And she couldn't bear it, couldn't bear him near her, yet couldn't bear him out of her sight either for fear of what he might be doing or even thinking.

Listening to Raul on the phone to Melina D'Agnolo had shattered her. Now, as he carried her past the superb flower arrangements which had appeared everywhere, and the frantically busy staff excited about the party which kicked off the weekend festivities, Polly felt like the weakest of the weak. No way was she going to be lying in bed this evening like a party pooper while Melina held the floor!

Raul set her upright in their bedroom. Confront him, screamed through her mind in letters of taunting fire. She walked over to the windows, torn by conflicting desires. She wanted to see them together first. She wanted to confront them. If she tried to confront Raul now, what did she base her accusations on? His appreciation of Melina's loy-

166

alty? Or that simple sentence 'I'm looking forward to see-ing you tonight'?

It wasn't enough. It wasn't evidence of anything he couldn't explain away. But the very fact he had been on the phone talking to Melina like that...it ripped Polly apart. She had genuinely trusted him, sincerely come to believe that it was only her own insecurity which was tormenting her...

'Do you think a married man needs a mistress?' she asked abruptly.

Silence stretched.

Polly spun round. Raul looked slightly bemused, a frown line etched between his expressive brows. Then a splinter-ing smile slashed his beautiful mouth. 'Not if he spends as much time in bed with his wife as I do!'

'It was a serious question, Raul.'

'Only not a very sensible one. With my background, the answer would be absolutely not. A divorce would be a bet-ter option,' Raul drawled reflectively.

Having invited that opinion, Polly's stomach curdled. She turned back to the windows on unsteady legs.

'Is there something you want to discuss with me?' Raul enquired in smooth invitation.

'Nothing.' Not without proof. She wasn't about to risk tearing their marriage apart without proper proof.

'I have this feeling that something is playing on your mind...it's not the first time I've had it.'

Taken aback by that assurance, Polly linked her unsteady hands tightly together and stared out of the window, seeing nothing. She might as well have been staring into space. Raul strolled to her side and followed the apparent path of her gaze.

Patrick Gorman was giving instructions to a group of workmen who were stringing up extra lighting in the gar-dens below.

'If I was the jealous type,' Raul breathed with sudden

startling rawness, 'I'd go down there and kill him because you're looking at him!'

Polly focused on Patrick for the first time in complete bewilderment, like someone who had missed a crucial sentence that made sense of inexplicable behaviour. 'I wasn't looking at him...why would I want to look at him, for heaven's sake?'

Raul punched the button that closed the curtains with what struck her as quite unnecessary force. Polly surveyed him. A devastatingly handsome male in a seething rage. She blinked. He strode out of the room without a backward glance.

He's jealous of Patrick. Polly slowly shook her head at that strikingly obvious revelation. Why hadn't she made that connection before? Right from the minute he had seen her chattering happily to the young Englishman Raul had been warning her off him. Yet how could he possibly be jealous of another man when he was planning to continue his affair with Melina?

But then wasn't that men the world over? she reflected with newly learnt cynicism. Some men only valued a woman when another man admired her, or when they thought that they themselves were no longer desired. And then a man could be possessive without loving. Which category did Raul fall into? Or was it simply that, as his wife, he now regarded her in the light of a possession?

She sank down on the edge of the bed, dry-eyed but pale as milk. Was Melina simply a habit with Raul? When he had told her that he appreciated her loyalty what had he meant? Had he been thanking her for patiently waiting for him? Did he honestly think he had a hope in hell of continuing such an affair without being found out?

The door opened again. Raul hovered for a split second, as if somewhat unsure of his welcome, and then extended his hand to her, one of his sudden flashing smiles driving all reserve from his lean bronzed features. 'We have a visitor, *gatita*,' he announced. 'My grandfather is here.'

Fidelio Navarro was stationed in the hall, curling his hat round and round between strained hands. Polly hurried down the stairs to greet him, breaking the ice by going straight up to him and leaning forward to kiss him on both cheeks, as one did with family members. He smiled and relaxed perceptibly while Raul translated her welcome with the air of a male grateful for the distraction.

Upstairs, Polly lifted Luis out of his cot and laid him in Fidelio's sturdy arms. The old man heaved a giant sigh and slowly shook his silvered head, openly overcome by the sight of his great-grandson.

'He says...Luis has my mother's eyes,' Raul translated gruffly.

Fidelio's eyes swam, his mouth tightening, his emotions too near the surface for him to say anything more. Polly accepted Luis back and looked at Raul hovering, her own gaze expectant. 'You go and have a celebration drink and talk now,' she instructed, knowing she had to spell it all out, afraid that, left to his own devices, Raul might duck the issue and take grateful refuge in polite conversation. 'You'll talk about your mother...and how much you loved her, and how good things are going to be now in this family.'

'*Sí...*' Raul dug his clenched fists tautly into his trouser pockets and bent his imperious dark head, swallowing hard.

Fidelio and Raul walked out of the room together about a foot apart.

Polly drew in a slow, deep breath and said a prayer that with a little give and take on both sides the barriers would finally come down between the two men. The older man needed to be completely sure of his welcome in this house. Without that confidence, he wouldn't visit again.

Two hours later, from the vantage point of an upper window, she watched Fidelio wrap his arms round Raul and hug him fiercely before he climbed back onto his horse outside the house. A tide of relief rolled over her. Clearly

Raul hadn't backed off and stood on his dignity. She was satisfied then.

'I wouldn't call them gifts,' Raul delivered some hours later, looking deadly serious in the reflection Polly could see of him in the mirror as she dazedly fingered the fabulous diamond necklace and earrings he had just presented her with. 'They belonged to my mother, so now they're yours.'

Polly stared down at the fabulous river of diamonds and the teardrop earrings with a lump in her throat. 'They're out of this world.'

Lifting the necklace, Raul clasped it round her throat. 'No one but me ever saw her wear them. My father never took her out in public.'

Polly gulped. 'Oh, heavens...that's so sad!'

'No, *mi esposa*.' Raul watched her put on the earrings and then stand up. 'We're a different generation, and the Zaforteza family has enjoyed a rebirth. I'm very grateful that the warmth I foolishly condemned you for has helped to heal the wounds of the past and persuade Fidelio to become a part of our lives.'

Wrinkling her nose to hold back tears in receipt of that surprisingly humble accolade, Polly turned to study her reflection in the cheval mirror. She looked elegant, with her hair swept up in a French roll, loose tendrils curling round her face. And then there was the dress, the designer sleeveless evening gown in green with the wonderful sweeping neckline and elaborate gilded embroidery, not to mention the spike-heeled shoes and all the diamonds catching fire under the lights. But none of that meant anything when set beside the burning sincerity she had glimpsed in Raul's stunning golden eyes. That filled her to bursting point with love.

Without the slightest warning, Raul reached for her hand and practically crushed the life from her fingers with the

unwitting fierceness of his grip. He exhaled in a stark hiss.
'I think I love you...'

Polly's eyes opened very wide, and then flooded with
pain. She hauled her fingers free in a gesture of repudiation.
'No, you don't. You're just feeling grateful and more emotional than usual,' she told him unevenly. 'Don't call that
love.'

'I said it wrong, but I haven't had a lot of practice at
this!' Raul gritted rawly. 'I shouldn't have said, I *think*—'

'You shouldn't have said anything. I'm sorry if I've
made you feel that nothing short of true love will satisfy
me,' Polly responded tautly, the stress and strain of the day
mounting up to betray her into saying exactly what she was
thinking. 'Actually, fidelity would do...so there, I've finally
lowered my expectations to a more realistic level!'

His fabulous bone structure prominent with tension beneath his bronzed skin, Raul dealt her a thunderous look of
disbelief that shook her. He parted his lips to respond at
the same moment that an urgent knock sounded on the
door.

'Our guests have begun to arrive,' he relayed seconds
later.

Before he could leave the room, Polly rushed over to
him, all cool abandoned in the growing awareness that she
had reacted in the worst possible way, her blue eyes deeply
troubled and full of guilt. 'Raul, I didn't mean...you took
me by—'

'Relax...you've cured me of my delusional state,' he derided, silencing her, convincing her that he could only have
spoken those words out of an impulsive need to reward her
in some way for helping to bring him and his grandfather
to a closer understanding.

It was not a good moment to go downstairs and discover
that Melina D'Agnolo had arrived with the first wave
of guests. Melina—spectacular in a glittering scarlet dress,
blonde hair gleaming and a brilliant smile on her ripe
pink mouth.

'What a lovely dress,' she said sweetly, and passed on.

Loads of baggage was being carried upstairs. Not everyone was staying the whole weekend, and not everyone was sleeping in the house. The equestrian centre had a spacious block of comfortable accommodation, used when Raul staged polo matches and occasional conferences, and many of their guests would be staying there. In the busy buzz of people, several different languages filling the air, Polly suffered a stark instant of panic, and then she drew in a deep, steadying breath and took her place at Raul's side.

Since being nice had never been a challenge for Polly—ironically with anyone but Raul—she soon found that natural friendliness was all that was required, and the approval in Raul's eyes soon dissolved her anxiety about socialising. Mid-way through the evening a fabulous fireworks display brought everyone out into the gardens. Polly was walking back indoors, hanging back to wait for Raul, who was chatting to a group of men, when Melina approached her.

'You watch him like an anxious mother, don't you?' It was an open sneer.

Polly coloured, suddenly painfully conscious that, whether she liked it or not, she *had* been sticking to Raul rather like superglue.

'Draped in diamonds worth millions,' Melina scorned with glittering green eyes. 'I hope they comfort you for sleeping alone at night.'

As Polly paled, the beautiful blonde flung her a triumphant look and strolled past her.

A pair of lean hands settled unexpectedly on her taut shoulders from behind. '*Dios mío*, how wonderfully friendly Melina's being!' Raul drawled above her slightly downbent head.

Polly jerked as if he had slapped her. 'Actually...'

'Actually?' Raul encouraged silkily.

'She was admiring my diamonds,' Polly completed dully.

'She's very fond of jewels...but not of her own sex.'

And who would know that best but him? That statement

only served to remind Polly that Raul had intimate knowledge of Melina's character. It made her feel more isolated than ever.

The musicians began to play the haunting country music of the *llanos* and one of them began to sing. 'What is he singing about?' she whispered.

'A broken heart…it may well be mine,' Raul breathed with stark impatience, releasing her to stride back indoors.

Did he care about Melina? *Really* care? Might he only have realised that after their marriage? Stranger things had happened, and she could not say that Raul was a male noticeably in touch with his own feelings except where Luis was concerned. So why had he told *her* that he thought he loved her?

As a reward? Those words were so easy to say. Out of guilt? Knowing that he was about to betray her, had he tossed that declaration at her like a consolation prize? Or to take the edge off any suspicions she might develop about his fidelity? And yet, strangely, that was the second time Raul had invited her to talk to him about what she had on her mind. Raul knew something was wrong. He had freely admitted that Melina didn't like her own sex, almost as if he didn't trust the beautiful blonde…

Any more than *you* trust *him*? That accidental comparison shocked Polly. For trust had been there until she'd overheard that phone call. And before that call, whenever she'd thought of telling Raul all the horrible things which Melina had slung at her, she had remembered that nasty little scene on the jet, and then the way he had walked out on her that same day after calling her obsessively jealous. Furthermore, she had no evidence of anything that Melina had said. Was she now trying to work herself up to running and telling tales like an immature little girl? Or was she seriously waiting for Raul to make some sort of move on Melina, who already seemed so unbearably smug tonight? Like a temporarily forsaken mistress aware that her star was now in the ascendant again?

Patrick wandered over to speak to her. 'I thought I'd avoid you while Raul was around,' he shared in an undertone, glancing rather anxiously around himself, like a man watching out for trouble.

'Why's that?'

'Raul is a Latin American male to his fingertips. I used to think he wasn't, except when he was being a killer on the polo field. Then he married you, and all of a sudden that cool front is cracking. I honestly don't think he can stand another man within twenty feet of you.'

'Really?' Polly lifted her head, a fledgling smile curving her lips because she was ready at that moment to snatch at any straw.

'So, if you don't mind, I won't ask you to dance.'

'No problem. I want to dance with Raul.' Polly drifted off, her mind made up. Time to stop avoiding the issue and allowing Melina to make her miserable and call all the shots. It was time to fight back and do the sensible thing, which was to talk to Raul.

So, in the mood she was in, it wasn't pleasant to find Raul, standing in a corner with a brooding look of darkness on his starkly handsome features, and Melina, chattering in that covert, intimate way she always embraced around him, her exquisite face soft with a cloying smile.

But Polly walked right over. 'Would you like to dance, Raul?' she asked in a rather high-pitched voice, and with a sudden spooky horror that he might say no and humiliate her.

Melina raised a brow and averted her eyes, a self-satisfied little smile playing about her lips. Raul strode forward, eyes blazing hot gold as they whipped over his wife's flushed and unhappy expression.

He closed an arm around her, and instead of taking her onto the floor to dance, he guided her out into the softly lit greater privacy of the gardens.

'I didn't really want to dance,' Polly admitted unevenly, wondering why on earth he should look so scorchingly an-

gry. 'I needed to talk to you in private. And if you're annoyed now, you're probably going to be even more annoyed when I've finished talking...so possibly we should
take a raincheck on this until later...'

Polly got two steps away, and then was unceremoniously
pulled back by the lean hand that closed round hers.

'No raincheck. You were saying?'

Polly breathed in deep to steady herself. She could not
say that harsh tone was the most inviting she had ever
heard. 'I heard you talking to Melina on the phone at the
villa—'

'Did you indeed?' Raul threw that query like a gauntlet.

It wasn't quite the response she had expected.

Polly became even more flustered. 'I want you to know
that up until that point I trusted you...and you may wonder
why I should say that, but, you see, Melina told me she
was your mistress the first day I came here, and she said
that you'd go back to her...and that night you *did* go over
there, and even though you *said* it was to see Fidelio—'

'One point at a time,' Raul intervened levelly. 'Melina
called me at the villa to inform me that, after wrestling with
her non-existent conscience, she had decided that it was her
duty to tell me that you were meeting up with Patrick
Gorman in secret.'

In shock at that news, Polly felt her mouth simply drop
open.

Raul dealt her a grim look of amusement. 'I thought that
would take the wind out of your sails.'

It did. Polly was poleaxed to realise that Melina had been
working on both her and Raul.

'Divide and conquer. Not very original or clever, at least
not clever enough to fool me,' Raul delineated grittily,
shooting Polly a forbidding glance of reproach. 'I didn't
believe a word of it, but I strung her along to see how far
she was prepared to go in her determination to cause trouble
between us. It also confirmed my suspicion that she had
been working on you as well.'

He hailed a passing maid with a snap of his fingers and spoke to her in Spanish.

'I want to know everything that Melina told you,' he said next, his lean, strong face hard and unyielding.

'Maybe you should pull up a chair. She said a lot,' Polly muttered uncertainly, suddenly not knowing whether she was on her head or her heels, and getting the horrendous feeling that every time she parted her lips she was digging another foot of her own grave. There was no doubt that the more Raul heard, the angrier he became.

'Her poison couldn't have fallen on more fertile ground,' Raul remarked grimly when she had finished speaking. 'That first night she joined us for dinner I watched her with you, and I was immediately suspicious of her behaviour. She was too friendly towards you and too flirtatious with me...you should have come straight to me with the truth. When you said nothing, I thought I might've misjudged her.'

Polly grimaced, suddenly feeling such a total idiot. 'I didn't want you to think I was jealous again.'

Firmly closing a determined hand over hers, Raul took her back indoors through the entrance that led into his suite of offices.

'How much proof do you need to trust me?' Raul challenged. 'We are about to face Melina together!'

At that disconcerting announcement, Polly gulped.

'I sent the maid to tell Melina that I wanted to see her in private.'

Raul thrust open the door before them. Melina was inside, lounging back against Raul's desk. She straightened with a bright smile that froze round the edges, her brow furrowing, when she saw Polly.

'After all the lies you've told, I'm amazed that you can look either of us in the face,' Raul drawled in icy condemnation.

Taken aback by that direct opening, Melina's eyes rounded. 'What are you—?'

'I've been more than fair to you,' Raul cut in. 'When you came to me last year, distraught about your financial problems, I was sympathetic.'

Two high spots of red now burned in Melina's cheeks. 'I wanted more than sympathy, Raul!'

'I paid you to act as my hostess when I entertained here. You were excellent in the role, but it was strictly a business arrangement.'

Melina's face twisted with fury. 'If it hadn't been for her and that wretched child we would've ended up with a lot more than a business arrangement—'

'There was never any question of that,' Raul dismissed with stark impatience. '*Dios mío*...I learned my lesson with you at nineteen, but I was willing to help you as a friend. The lies you've fed Polly...and attempted to feed me...merely prove that you haven't changed at all, Melina.'

'I don't know what you *see* in her!' Melina raged at him incredulously. '*I* should have been your wife!'

'You wouldn't know love if it smacked you in the face,' Raul responded with contempt. 'Greed and ambition are no more attractive to me now than they were years ago.'

Melina reddened, sent him a look of loathing, and then seemed to collect herself. Tossing her head high, she parted her lips, but Raul got in first. 'I expect you to vacate your present accommodation by the end of the month. I won't be renewing the lease and you are no longer welcome here. A car will take you home.'

Without another word, Raul swept Polly back out of the room. Her legs felt hollow and butterflies were dancing in her tummy. She could not credit what a fool she had been to listen to the other woman's insidious lies. 'She's *never* been your mistress...'

'We had a brief affair when I was nineteen,' Raul admitted grimly. 'Although I didn't know it, I was far from being her only lover at the time. She's several years older than me. I *was* infatuated with her, but I wasn't a complete fool. Melina couldn't hide her greed. No matter what I gave her, she wanted more. When she realised I had no plans to marry her, she married a wealthy industrialist in his sixties—'

'And he died?'

'No, she's been married twice. Her first husband divorced her; the second died, leaving her in debt.'

'And that's when she came to you for help?'

Raul nodded, his jawline squaring. 'I should've known better than to take pity on her, *gatita*. She was always a bitch.'

'She resented me…she was just furious that you'd married me…'

'*Dios mío*, I didn't even realise that she was hoping I might become involved with her again. I'm not attracted to her now, but she can be amusing company.'

'I've been an idiot,' Polly mumbled ruefully.

'I should've made you tell me the truth. Your silence protected her.'

They returned to the party. Polly was light-headed with relief but thoroughly humbled by the awareness that she had been very naive in her dealings with Melina, and that it had taken Raul to sort it all out. OK, she had finally surrendered to the need to tell him the truth, but it had taken her too long to reach that point.

She wanted so much to be alone with Raul then, but it was impossible with so many people around. It was near dawn before the last of their guests dispersed. By then Polly felt stressed out emotionally, riven with guilt that she had so misjudged Raul and appalled that he knew of the suspicions she had cherished. And, worst of all, how could she have reacted as she had when he'd talked about loving her? Hadn't he already shown in lots of ways that he cared about her, desired her, enjoyed her company? So maybe that still didn't quite amount to her estimation of love, but it was probably as close as she was likely to get to being loved!

Raul thrust the bedroom door shut behind him, his screened gaze zeroing in on her aimless stance in the middle of the carpet. 'I wish every one of our guests would evaporate,' he admitted with real fervour.

'But—'

'No buts, *mi esposa*, privacy is at a premium this weekend, but thankfully we're leaving for London on Sunday evening. I have a surprise for you. Monday *is* your birthday,' Raul reminded her.

'London…a *surprise*?' Polly's cup of guilt positively overflowed. 'I'm really sorry I listened to Melina.'

'You didn't know what you were up against.' Reaching for her, Raul eased her slowly into the circle of his arms. 'And now it's time for you to keep quiet and listen to me.'

Polly gazed up into clear dark golden eyes and her susceptible heart quickened.

'I fell in love with you in Vermont,' Raul delivered almost aggressively, strain hardening his sensual mouth. 'But I didn't realise that until recently. I basked in your response to me then. You asked nothing from me, but your love made you feel as much mine as the baby you carried.'

Polly was transfixed. 'Did it?'

'I felt very possessive of you even then. I'm not prone to analysing my emotions…I didn't have to,' Raul admitted bluntly. 'When you went missing, you went missing with my baby inside you, so I never had to question the strength of my need to find you both. I was always able to use Luis as a justification. And when I found it a challenge to keep our relationship impersonal, I told myself it was solely because you were the mother of my child.'

'You were pretty good at convincing yourself,' Polly whispered unevenly, almost afraid to believe in what he was trying to explain to her.

'I even had a good excuse to marry you—'

'I forced you into it.'

'I could've said no, and I didn't. You made it easy for me to avoid facing up to the fact that I wanted you on any terms…and then you vanished and I was climbing the walls with frustration again,' Raul confessed, and shifted a shoulder in a jerky shrug that signified unpleasant recollection. 'I was angrier than I've ever been in my life, and yet so scared that I wouldn't be able to find you a second time…'

She rested her brow against his broad chest, disturbed that she had caused him that much pain without even suspecting the fact. 'Oh, Raul…I thought it was only Luis you'd be worrying about and missing.'

'I didn't know what was happening inside my own head,' he confided grittily. 'I even assumed that once I'd satisfied my overpowering desire to make love to you I would go back to feeling like myself again. But it didn't work like that.'

'It doesn't,' Polly agreed shakily, eyes stinging with happiness because believing that Raul loved her was becoming easier with every word he spoke.

'When I came back in from that late-night ride and you weren't where I expected you to be I really lost it, and that's when I realised how much power you had over me…that was a very threatening discovery for me,' Raul conceded with driven honesty. 'And then it got worse…'

'*Worse?*' Falling in love wasn't always fun, but Raul was making it sound like being plunged into hell.

'With women, it was always easy come, easy go with me, and then you smiled at Patrick Gorman just the way you once smiled at me in Vermont, and I wanted to knock his teeth down his throat! It was so irrational, so childish, *querida*,' he grated, with a highly revealing combination of regret and embarrassment.

'I didn't really notice…I was too busy worrying about Melina and my own insecurities.' Polly winced at how blind she had been.

'It slowly dawned on me that this was what love felt like…all these crazy feelings, and rage and moments of weakness and fear, and just needing you there all the time…' His sculpted cheekbones were sharpened by a rise of dark colour. '*Infierno*…I can't believe I just said all that!'

'But it's like that for me too, and, believe me, loving you was not fun when we met up in London again, so I tried to tell myself I hated you,' Polly complained feelingly, but she wrapped her arms round him so tightly when she said it he wasn't in any danger of feeling rejected on the basis of his past sins.

'I wanted to haul you into my arms and I couldn't let myself…and now I can,' Raul appreciated, with a blazing smile of satisfaction and relief. He crushed her to him and proceeded to kiss her until her head swam. They ended up on the bed, discarding clothes with more haste than finesse, sealing their words of love with a passionate joining that released every last scrap of tension between them.

'Yes, you *do* like being loved,' Polly teased him as she smoothed possessive fingers through his damply tousled hair and met the tender look of satisfaction in his brilliant dark eyes.

'You should've guessed how I felt at the villa, *gatita*. I don't think I've ever felt that happy before…except now,' he conceded reflectively.

'Why are we going to London?'

'Surprise…'

'But I'm curious…' Polly ran a not entirely innocent hand down over a lean, hair-roughened thigh.

Raul gave her a wolfish grin even as he hauled her closer. 'You could torture me and I wouldn't tell you!'

'Am I going to be pleased?'

'You're worse than a child,' Raul groaned with vibrant amusement, and glanced at his watch. 'Are you aware that we have to rise to be hosts again in two hours?'

Polly was aghast.

'And if I fall asleep on El Lobo's back during the polo match, guess who I'm likely to blame?'

'It's only a game,' she said comfortingly.

Lowering his head, Raul studied her with frankly adoring but slightly pained eyes. 'I must be in love. Once I'd have slaughtered any woman for saying that…'

\*    \*    \*

'Why are you bringing me here?' Polly exclaimed three days later as the limousine wafted them up the long drive-way to Gilbourne, her late godmother's beautiful Georgian house in Surrey.

'Happy birthday. I bought Gilbourne months ago. A whim. Don't ask me why... I came here looking for you and I remembered how much you'd talked about this place in Vermont. The estate agent was showing the most ob-noxious couple round the grounds, and they were giving forth about how they would rip out the rose garden where you used to sit with your godmother.'

It took Polly the entirety of that speech to catch her breath. 'You bought it for *me*?'

'When we come to England we can stay here,' Raul pointed out.

Polly was staring out at the other limousine already parked in front of the house, and then her eyes widened even more at the sight of the helicopter on the front lawn.

'Who's here?'

'Your friends, Maxie and Darcy—'

'Maxie and Darcy?' Polly gasped, barely over the first shock of discovering that she was now the owner of the gorgeous mansion she had always adored visiting as a child.

'I did try to bring them over for the fiesta, but Maxie's pregnant, and couldn't face the prospect of a long flight, so I decided to arrange the reunion here.'

Polly was touched, but she had also paled with dismay. 'Raul...the last time I was in the same room with Maxie and Darcy it was like holding off World War Three. We all used to be great friends, and then three years ago it all went wrong. Darcy was getting married and Maxie was her bridesmaid, and Darcy's bridegroom fell head over heels for Maxie. Relations have been strained ever since.'

'But not so strained that they weren't both prepared to come here to see you,' Raul countered reassuringly.

And, minutes after walking into the gracious drawing

room where all three women had last met for the reading of Nancy Leeward's will, Polly was engulfed by a very warm welcome from her friends. Both Maxie and Darcy were chattering nineteen to the dozen—to her, to *each other*, and throwing stray comments in the direction of the men in the background.

'I recognise Angelos from his photo,' Polly whispered. 'But who's the other one?'

'My husband, Luca,' Darcy announced with lashings of pride. 'Gianluca Raffacani. He's Zia's father.'

Since Polly had entirely the wrong idea about who had fathered Darcy's little daughter, those twin announcements left her fairly bereft of speech.

'They're all listening, scared they're missing something. Look, what do you say we dump the men for half an hour?' Maxie suggested in a covert whisper.

So off they went on a supposed tour of the house. And Polly heard about how Darcy had called Maxie and had lunch with her a couple of weeks earlier.

'We made up,' Darcy completed.

Polly beamed. 'That's brilliant. So, congratulations on your marriage...and I hear you're pregnant, Maxie?'

'Never been so sick in my life,' Maxie moaned, her beautiful face a tinge paler than was the norm. 'But it should pass off in a couple of weeks. It'll be worth it if I land a cute little sprog like Luis.'

They stood looking down on the rose garden where they had often sat with their godmother, and finally settled in a row on the window seat.

'Do you think Nancy's pleased with us now?' Darcy said hopefully.

Maxie grinned. 'She did me a favour...I got Angelos.'

'Luca's changed my life,' Darcy confided.

Both women looked at Polly, and she went pink. 'Raul's fabulous.'

'Oh, *no*!' Maxie groaned with a comical expression of

dismay. 'I just know the men think we're up here talking about them, and here we are actually doing it!'

Hours later, Polly climbed into the elegant, beautifully draped four-poster bed in the main bedroom, marvelling that Raul had simply bought the furniture with the house and engaged new staff. He hadn't worked it out yet, but she knew what had been going through his mind all those months ago. He had walked around Gilbourne, imagining her here, and he had bought the house as a result.

'So what *were* the three of you giggling like drains over?' Raul persisted as he slid into bed beside her, all bronzed and gorgeous and sexy against the pale linen.

Pulses quickening, Polly gave him a secretive smile. 'That would be telling.'

'You were talking about us.' Raul lay back against the banked up pillows, his trust in that belief complete. '*We* talked business.'

'Get away—you were in the billiard room by the time we came back, but you hadn't closed the door, so we tiptoed up to see how the three of you were getting on without us around,' Polly confessed with a growing smile. 'And Angelos was talking about what a great mother Maxie was going to be, Luca was talking about Darcy's amazing knowledge of antiques. And *you* were talking about my inborn talent for horse-riding!'

Raul rolled over and trapped her beneath him, stunning golden eyes laughing down into hers. 'I may have exaggerated a little, but then it was male bragging session, and I couldn't say what I really wanted to say...'

'And what was that?' Polly enquired, scarcely able to breathe for excitement with him that close.

'I just adore you, *gatita*...'

'Me too.' Polly sighed ecstatically as he kissed her, closed her eyes the way she always did, and gave herself up without a care in the world to loving pleasure.

Look for a new and exciting series from Harlequin!

HARLEQUIN
*Duets*™

*Two __new__ full-length novels in
one book, from some of your
favorite authors!*

Starting in May, each month we'll
be bringing you two new books,
each book containing two brand-
new stories about the lighter side of
love! Double the pleasure, double
the romance, for less than the cost
of two regular romance titles!

Look for these two new
Harlequin Duets™ titles
in May 1999:

Book 1:
WITH A STETSON AND A SMILE
by Vicki Lewis Thompson
THE BRIDESMAID'S BET
by Christie Ridgway

Book 2:
KIDNAPPED? by Jacqueline Diamond
I GOT YOU, BABE by Bonnie Tucker

**2 GREAT
STORIES BY
2 GREAT
AUTHORS
FOR 1 LOW
PRICE!**

*Don't miss it! Available May 1999 at your
favorite retail outlet.*

HARLEQUIN®
*Makes any time special.*™

Look us up on-line at: http://www.romance.net        HDGENR

# Coming Next Month

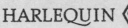 

## HARLEQUIN PRESENTS®

### THE BEST HAS JUST GOTTEN BETTER!

**#2019 PACIFIC HEAT Anne Mather**
Olivia was staying with famous film star Diane Haran to write her biography, despite the fact that Diane had stolen Olivia's husband. Now Olivia planned to steal Diane's lover, Joe Castellano, by seduction...for revenge!

**#2020 THE MARRIAGE DECIDER Emma Darcy**
Amy had finally succumbed to a night of combustible passion with her impossibly handsome boss, Jake Carter. Now things were back to business as usual; he was still a determined bachelor...and she was pregnant....

**#2021 A VERY PRIVATE REVENGE Helen Brooks**
Tamar wanted her revenge on Jed Cannon, the notorious playboy who'd hurt her cousin. She'd planned to seduce him, then callously jilt him—but her plan went terribly wrong: soon it was marriage she wanted, not vengeance!

**#2022 THE UNEXPECTED FATHER Kathryn Ross**
(Expecting!)
Mom-to-be Samantha Walker was looking forward to facing her new life alone—but then she met the ruggedly handsome Josh Hamilton. But would they ever be able to overcome their difficult pasts and become a real family?

**#2023 ONE HUSBAND REQUIRED! Sharon Kendrick**
(Wanted: One Wedding Dress)
Ross Sheridan didn't know that his secretary, Ursula O'Neill, was in love with him until his nine-year-old daughter, Katie, played matchmaker.... Then it was only a matter of time before Katie was Ross and Ursula's bridesmaid!

**#2024 WEDDING FEVER Lee Wilkinson**
Raine had fallen in love with Nick Marlowe, not knowing the brooding American was anything but available. Years later, she was just about to marry another man when Nick walked back into Raine's life. And this time, he *was* single!